A
FULL
MOON
OF
WOMEN

ALSO BY URSULE MOLINARO

NOVELS

Green Lights Are Blue

Sounds of a Drunken Summer

The Borrower

Encores for a Dilettante

The Autobiography of Cassandra, Princess & Prophetess of Troy

Positions with White Roses

Remnants of an Unknown Woman, the original trash novel, with collage
drawings by John Evans

The New Moon with the Old Moon in Her Arms

STORY COLLECTIONS

Bastards: Footnotes to History

Nightschool for Saints

Top Stories #16

Needlepoint

13

A

FULL

MOON

OF

WOMEN

29 Word Portraits of Notable Women

from Different Times & Places + 1 Void of Course

URSULE MOLINARO

DUTTON / NEW YORK

DUTTON
Published by the Penguin Group
Penguin Books USA Inc., 375 Hudson Street,
New York, New York 10014, U.S.A.
Penguin Books Ltd, 27 Wrights Lane,
London W8 5TZ, England
Penguin Books Australia Ltd, Ringwood,
Victoria, Australia
Penguin Books Canada Ltd, 2801 John Street,
Markham, Ontario, Canada L3R 1B4
Penguin Books (N.Z.) Ltd, 182–190 Wairau Road,
Auckland 10, New Zealand

Penguin Books Ltd, Registered Offices:
Harmondsworth, Middlesex, England

First published by Dutton, an imprint of Penguin Books USA Inc.

First printing, July, 1990
10 9 8 7 6 5 4 3 2 1

Library of Congress Cataloging-in-Publication Data
Molinaro, Ursule.
    A full moon of women : 29 word portraits of notable women from
different times & places : + 1 void of course / Ursule Molinaro. —
1st ed.
        p. cm.
    ISBN 0-525-24848-X
    I. Title.
PS3525.02152F85   1990
813'.54—dc20   90-30077

Printed in the United States of America
Set in Plantin Light
Designed by Ann Gold

These stories originally appeared in the following publications: "Cassandra," as part
of the novel *The Autobiography of Cassandra, Princess & Prophetess of Troy* (Archer
Press, 1980); "Charlotte Corday," a PEN Syndicated Fiction Project selection in *The
San Francisco Chronicle* and *The Village Advocate* (1985); "Simone Weil" in
Formations (1986); "Mary Maclane" in *Hawaii Review* (1987); "Stellina (Remnants
of an Unknown Woman)" as a limited edition (Red Dust, 1987); "Clara Schumann"
in *Edinburgh Review* (1988); and "Hypatia" in *Hypatia, A Journal of Feminist
Philosophy* (1989). "Lise Meitner," "Zenobia," "Frida Kahlo," "Ka'ahumanu,"
"Mu-Lan Hwa," "Ottoline Morell," "Adèle Hugo," "Marie Laveau," and "Snow
White" were all published by James Mechem in *Redstart* and *Caprice*; they have
become his dedicated women.

Many of the women who compose this *Full Moon* were suggested to me by their posthumous fans. I therefore wish to dedicate:

CHARLOTTE CORDAY to Sandra Pearlman

LISE MEITNER to Barbara Gramann

ZENOBIA to Valerie Wayne

JOAN OF ARC to Rebecca Lee

OLYMPE DE GOUGES to Micheline Beuve

KA'AHUMANU to Larene Despain

BETSY STOCKTON to Frank Stewart

MADGE TENNENT to Nell Alteizer

HYPATIA to Dion Farquhar

SUZANNE VALADON to Martin Davis (in memoriam)

CLARA SCHUMANN to Bruce Benderson

MU-LAN HWA to Terri Goto

SIMONE WEIL to Daile Kaplan

STELLINA to John Evans

OTTOLINE MORELL to Robert Martin

FANNY KEMBLE to Robert Martin

ALEXANDRA DAVID-NEEL to Barbara & Michael Foster

MARY MACLANE to Alice Loftin

ADÈLE HUGO to Pamela Gay

MARIE LAVEAU to Léon Viard de Saint Laurent (in memoriam)
     & Bruce Benderson

SNOW WHITE to Cristina Bacchilega

CONTENTS

A
FULL
MOON
OF
WOMEN

INTRODUCTION
SISTERS IN
IRONY

CHARLOTTE CORDAY was a heroine of my adolescence. I identified with her secret determination: to leave home without telling her parents. With her friendlessness, which matched my own at 13, though no longer at 25, when she committed the murder that made her "historical."

I admired the precision of her single lethal blow —which may have been luck; mainly for her victim.— & the logic of her brilliant useless self-defense in court.

I often wondered how she felt, sitting in her cell waiting to be guillotined, after being told that the man she had killed at the price of her life barely had 3 more months to live.

The irony of her well-planned, almost gratuitous act of courage gave me the idea to look into the lives of other women, whose talents, unusual (usually unwomanly) interests, & dedications singled them out for notice by their contemporaries. —Rarely for their admiration, sometimes for posthumous apology &/or sanctification.

The most obvious second was Charlotte Corday's acknowledged role model JOAN OF ARC.   —Burned alive not so much for the unorthodoxy of her religious & patriotic fervor, as for the heresy of wearing men's clothes: her armor.

She was soon followed by others whose accomplishments & sacrifices seemed to have had about as much effect as certain Civil War cannonballs allegedly stopped in their course by wash (sheets & blankets) hung out to dry.

HYPATIA   —a Greek philosopher, dismembered alive by a mob of Christians.

LISE MEITNER   —whose early successes with uranium fission went ignored or ridiculed by the press. Until Hiroshima & Nagasaki prompted reporters to interview the aged nuclear physicist; implying that she had started it all.

FRIDA KAHLO   —carried on a stretcher to the opening of her first one-woman show.

KA'AHUMANU   —the most powerful Hawaiian queen, who abolished the eating taboos that had been fatal for transgressing women. Who told the first New England missionaries that she & her people had just gotten rid of their old gods, & needed no new ones. But then died an ardent Calvinist, baptized Elizabeth.

LUCY GOODALE THURSTON   —a New England missionary, unchanged by 48 years in Hawaii.

EMMA HALE SMITH   —a crusader's crusader, victimized by one of her prophet's incidental principles: polygamy.

FRANCES MILTON TROLLOPE   —maligned & ridiculed as a writer, eclipsed by the son she raised on her writing.

SIMONE WEIL   —crystal-clear intelligence, smoke-screened by pain.

CARO(LINE) LAMB   —slighted for being slight.

MARY MACLANE   —a one-year celebrity, found dead in a fleabag hotel, the clippings of her strawfire fame neatly arranged around her.

CASSANDRA   —female intelligence punished for spurning the most beautiful of the gods.

STELLINA   —a lonely immigrant, praying at Lourdes in the Bronx to be promoted from fruit packer to tomato packer.

FANNY KEMBLE   —an American marriage transforms a star of the London stage into a militant writer against slavery.

ADÈLE HUGO   —a fine watercolorist & wit, who became a wife, & nothing but a wife.

OLYMPE DE GOUGES   —famous for her last words: If women can mount the scaffold (to be guillotined), they can also mount the rostrum (to speak their minds).

There are also a few successes & seeming fulfillments:

MADGE TENNENT   —was recognized as a painter (mainly of Hawaiian women) during the last third of her life.

QUEEN ZENOBIA   —remained a respected ruler even in defeat.

MADAME BLAVATSKY   —is still the subject of the ardent controversy that raged during her lifetime: the greatest mystic/the greatest imposter. The greatest either way.

ALICE NEEL   —came into her "own" around 80.

ALEXANDRA DAVID-NEEL   —lived to be a serene 101, after risking her life at least as many times.

MARIE LAVEAU   —knew years of absolute triumph as a Voodoo queen.

BETSY STOCKTON   —an ex-slave, became the embodiment of the privilege of education.

But minor ironies exist also among the apparently successful:

MARIE LAURENCIN   —was "chic" as a painter, & free as a woman, but art critics dropped her when she dropped her lover Apollinaire.

CLARA SCHUMANN   —came to believe that composing

music was a talent reserved for men, after she married Schumann.

SUZANNE VALADON   —was recognized as a painter, but became better known as the mother of her alcoholic genius son Maurice Utrillo.

OTTOLINE MORELL   —loved many of the writers & artists she discovered & helped, but they made fun of her for being tall & rich.

MU-LAN HWA   —rid China of Mongolian invaders, disguised in the general's uniform of her father, who was too old to go to war. As a reward, the emperor offered her one of his daughters in marriage.

Many of the 29 women who make up this *Full Moon* were suggested to me by the persons to whom they are dedicated. They are 29 women from different civilizations & social backgrounds. They have different educations, different ambitions, different visions of reality. They are factory workers, queens, peasant girls, princesses, philosophers, artists, writers, scientists, actresses, mystics, world travelers; virgins, mothers, renowned lovers, wives.

They are dead now, but need to be resurrected to become as desirable as the thirtieth woman, the sole survivor at the end: the indestructible Snow White, whose docile beauty mocks their active, often daring, rebellious lives.

THE
HISTORICAL
WEEK OF
CHARLOTTE
CORDAY
D'ARMONT

July 13, 1793, 7 P.M., & after

Does killing a killer make you a killer. Or are you a hero on the contrary, a dragon slayer, a saint, fulfilling a mission.

Even if the killer you kill looks like a hero/a dragon slayer/a political saint —long suffering with migraines & skin cancer— to the majority of your contemporary countrymen. Frenchmen, who can, of course be wrong when they call you: a murderess. An assassin.

Like the mongoloid servant who hits you over the head with the handle of his broom when he finds you wandering through the rooms of your victim's house, away from the room of your deed.

Who holds on to your ample breasts, to make sure you don't get away, until more resourceful revolutionaries rush in from the street, & tie you to a chair.

A delicate chair, with red satin arm rests & fluted royal legs, on which your victim used to sit, signing executions. Until the pain of his rotting skin became everpresent, intolerable, & he could endure sitting only in lukewarm water, in a stubby copper tub, signing executions on a board balanced on the tub's edges.

5

Like your victim's physician. Who calls you: needlessly impatient. & tells you: that you might have spared yourself the trouble   & your body the just loss of its head   & your conscience the guilt   & your respectable parents the shame, had you consulted him beforehand. You stabbed a dying man: he tells you, with the omniscient sarcasm of the medical profession: You spared your victim 3 months of pain. Which was all the time he had left to live on this earth. At most.

Like the red-faced mob that surrounds your victim's house. Jeering. Leering at the torn bodice of your Sunday best, in which you'd dressed to look receivable. To the woman who answers the door of your intended victim. Whom you reassure with your beauty.

You're almost dismembered, as you squeeze through the thicket of fists & reaching hands, behind the shielding body of your arresting officer. Who leads you to the coach that takes you to prison.

July 17, 1793, 11 A.M., & after

Like your prosecutor, who holds up the 6-inch carving knife
    by the tip, not by its ebony handle   which you purchased on the morning of your deed. & had the merchant hone to razor sharpness before you paid him for it.

Who expresses surprise at the skill of your single lethal blow. & shocks you, suggesting that you must be practiced in this kind of craft. "The Monster," you whisper, "he thinks I'm an assassin."

Like your defense lawyer, who pleads that you're insane. That your convent-educated classical mind is clouded with political fanaticism.

As the court instructed him to plead. Because the 3 days you spent in prison threaten to change you from a political assassin to a martyr. & the other   as yet still living   leaders of the revolution have begun to fear you more than they feared all the still living   monarchists of France.

After you calmly state your reason for your deed: That you believed in Equality, Brotherhood, & Freedom, & had been a republican since long before the revolution. Which you had felt compelled to serve. Setting aside your private needs to serve the need of your country. Which you *had* served, with your deed.

Astounding those who hear you by the clear logic & presence of your mind.

But not like your prison guards. Who weep as you make them a present of your long radiant chestnut hair. Which you insist on cutting off yourself. Before you slip into the flimsy red cotton smock in which condemned assassins ride to their execution.

Or your executioner, who rides with you in the cart. & tries to block the guillotine as it looms into view when your cart turns the corner of rue Royale.

You've never seen one before, & you politely ask the man to move aside a little. You want to know what the thing looks like. Considering the position you're in, you're understandably curious, you say to him, with a line of a smile.

Impressing your executioner. Who feels that he's escorting the statue of a heroine, as a sudden cloudburst sculpts your classic contours, under the drapery of wet red cotton.

Or the huge silent crowd that watches you climb the scaffold. & begins to cheer your stately ascent. & even throws you roses. Which are the last thing you see on this earth: roses, lying on the planks at your feet, as you embrace the wood under the blade.

But again like the hired helper. Who holds up your head by one ear, & gives it a punch. Making your severed face blush at the outrage.

Which outrages also many of your spectators. They begin to boo the hired helper, who hastily places your head in the basket.

July 18, 1793

& again like Jacques-Louis David, the painter of heroes, & officially appointed Art Dictator of the French Revolution. Who performs the autopsy on your headless classical body. & informs the world: That you died a virgin.

Before he paints Jean-Paul Marat, one of the great leaders of the French Revolution   your stabbed victim   in the act of dying.

Before he paints Napoleon Bonaparte. & Napoleon Bonaparte's horse. With the technique of admiration that sends him into exile (to Bruxelles), but not to the guillotine, after his painted heroes fall from public grace.

Before the historical week of your life becomes the legend of: Charlotte Corday.

The formally educated only daughter of impoverished aristocrats. Great-niece of the great Pierre Corneille, who invented morally motivated French tragedy. Which centuries of French schoolchildren are forced to recite. Which they learn, groaning for lack of moral motivation. Avenging their boredom by calling your great-uncle, the great Corneille: *Cette grande corneille . . .* (That old crow . . .)

Before your radiant chestnut hair becomes a relic, which your surviving prison guards sell in thin strands at high prices. Before the cleft in your chin becomes symbolic of the determination with which you set out   an older, better-born, better-educated, intellectual Joan of Arc, the best-looking young woman in all of Normandy   on July 10, 1793, at daybreak, to walk the 200 miles from Caen   (famous for its "tripes," its dish of guts)   to Paris. Carrying one change of clothes: the Sunday best you planned to wear to conceal the purpose of your visit in the disguise of beauty. & respectability.

It is a 3-day walk, but you're robust, in excellent health, a 25-year-old virgin with a classically educated passion for reason.

Which fans your hatred for Jean-Paul Marat, the mad scientist

turned witch hunter, for killing off the best minds of his &
your revolution.

You've told no one where you're going, or what you plan to
do when you get there. Your secret mission has been ripening
inside you like a fetus, which might abort if you air it with words.
Besides, you've made no intimate friends, during the 25 years of
your life.

You do not say goodbye to your parents. Whom you might not
be able to convince that you're another Joan of Arc. Your relationship with them is formal politeness, & the political discussions
you've had with them have always condemned fanaticism. Even
if your mother seemed to share your feelings when she suggested
that: Your eventual victim had been turned inside out by his skin
disease. That his rotting flesh was the outward manifestation of
his acid cruelty.

Before the choice of your hotel Hôtel de la Providence becomes the subject of speculation by students of history: Had you hoped to enlist the help of providence, or thought
yourself its messenger.

Which is how you, the guillotined assassin of one of the great
leaders of the French Revolution, have begun to look to the posthumous centuries of schoolchildren who groaningly recite your
great, great-uncle's tragedies.

From which you step: a heroine, your beauty amply matched
by moral motivation. A credit to your otherwise unheard-of parents. An ardent patriot of peace, with farseeing wide grey eyes.
From the courageous province of Normandy, where winter sea-
gulls move inland, littering the landscape like bottled snow.

APPLESAUCE:
FROM THE
FALL TO
FALLOUT

LISE
MEITNER

November 7, 1878–
October 27, 1968

Hiroshima happens. & Nagasaki. Science shocks the war to a stop. & suddenly a broadcaster at an American radio station thinks of: Lise Meitner. The Austrian physicist who experimented with uranium fission. Wasn't she the first to split the atom.   —Another Eve nibbling on forbidden knowledge. Passing the core on to Adam.—   Let's do a transatlantic radio interview with this senior lady scientist in her Stockholm retreat. Let's find out how she feels about the recent consequence of her discoveries.

—About a Japanese girl   a little girl, born just about the time of the first realized split   standing dazed in a landscape of splinters. Raising one hand to touch a strangeness in her cheek. Feeling her fingers go through the melted side of her face.—

Hello? Yes, I can hear you very loud.

But you surprise me. I don't know what you want me to say, in my bad English. Your interview confuses me. I'm not used to being given individual credit for my discoveries. Most of my experiments were joint ventures. With (male) colleagues better known than I.   —& I'm not thinking only of Einstein.—

Most of my papers were written in collaboration, co-signed. We all worked together. Nobody was racing to be first.

I don't remember being first in anything. I started my life as the third of seven siblings.

We were Jews, but my parents were free-thinkers, & had us baptized as Protestants.   —Perhaps they liked the semantic implication of protest in what they thought to be the least meddlesome of official religions in late-19th-century Austria.

Still, I've been a wandering Jew most of my life. A wanderer luckier than many of my race chosen for homelessness. I found a home in science.

As early as 1901 I found it, when I was 23. When my parents reluctantly abandoned their hopes of making me into a self-supporting teacher of French, & allowed me to enroll in the science department at the University of Vienna.   —Although, at that time, I still thought I *had* a home. In Vienna.—   Again, I was not the first woman to receive a doctorate in science there. I was the second.

& considered a freak as much as the first. A young lady interested in physics. In Vienna of all places. A city specializing in ladylike young ladies.

Berlin was not much better. When I gave my inaugural lecture on cosmic physics there in 1922, it was reported as "cosmetic" physics by the press.

Insulting my colleagues more than me. By then I'd grown used to the media's discomfort at the thought   let alone the sight of a nuclear physicist in a skirt. By then, the thrill of watching some of my intuitions prove true   —after years of photographing electrons; the most reliable method, in my experience— far outweighed the (s)wordplay of men whose scientific curiosity seemed to have stopped with the birds & the bees.

How could they be expected to understand the thrill of prying open one of the basic laws of the universe. Whose application to everyday living was bound to improve life for everybody. The thought that this discovery might be used for military purpose that it might be turned into an instrument of boundless devastation never entered my mind. —Which is the mind of a woman, after all, perhaps, in that respect. With a biological inclination to nurture.— Although I'm sure Prometheus thought only that he was bringing light & warmth, when he shared the gods' secret of making fire with human beings.

Who then used this gift for the destruction of other human beings. I also have the mind of a Jew. Historically programmed to think: victim, when I'm asked to think of military purposes.

—When Hitler annexed Austria, I became a legal nonentity. One of the few of my endangered species allowed to leave Berlin with a private destination. By the grace of my work, which I had to leave behind. But which my compatriots of my privileged new homeland of science had come to recognize, & judged worthy of survival. A valid physicist with an invalidated Austrian passport, I was allowed to wander from Holland to Denmark & eventually to Sweden, where I was invited to resume my work at the Nobel Institute in Stockholm.

I was 60 then.

—& rewarded with the irrefutable proof that the two mutually repulsed nuclear fragments would be driven apart as I had calculated. It all fit. We had split the atom.—

But I refused my colleagues' invitation to join their teamwork on the development of a nuclear fission bomb. I wrote a last brief comment on the asymmetry of fission fragments, & withdrew.

I don't understand why what happened to Hiroshima & Nagasaki makes you think of me. I don't know what to make of this unexpected transatlantic interview. Of your sudden interest in a retired physicist. Whom you're overwhelming with sudden credit for having stumbled onto something that produced a holocaust.

Something that may eventually produce the end of humanity.

Whoever made you think that I'd be thrilled by a surprise hello, at the end of your broadcast, from my Americanized sister. Who asks: Tell me something, Lise. Do you still not know how to cook?

A VIRTUOUS WOMAN

ZENOBIA, QUEEN OF PALMYRA

3rd century A.D.   Picture a noble adolescent girl, descended from the kings of Egypt. She has the keen eyes of birds of prey. As unsmiling. The pleasing line of her nose curves lightly above the fine line of the mouth. Also unsmiling, despite the whitest teeth. Her hair is dark blue, & straight. It frames her noble head like a glistening helmet.

Now drape the noble adolescent body in the pelt of a lion, slain & skinned with her own sand-colored hands. Arm her with a spear & a sword, & follow her   if you dare   up & down mountains, through villages & thickets, until exhaustion.

She lies down under a tree & falls asleep.

An early-risen bear passes on his way to the village he has been terrorizing. He stops & nuzzles Zenobia's ankles. She leaps to her feet & wrestles him to the ground. Then she drags his lifeless body through the village.

Where she inspires greater fear than the bear. But also admiration. & romantic love.

Which she shrugs off. In anger: Repulsed by the thought of

her independent body pinned beneath a man. She wishes to remain a virgin for life.

Distressing her parents, who wish for grandchildren. From a daughter whom they beg to lay down her arms.

Whom they raised to be an accomplished woman, her physical prowess amply matched by learning. A woman well versed in the letters of her time. Tutored in philosophy by the wise Longinus. She is fluent in Latin & in Greek.

Parental pressure & filial obedience finally force her to consent to marry the King of Palmyra. Odenathus, a pleasing specimen of his sex, both in face & in body. She is sure to produce pleasing children with him.

Which she does.

Pleasing her parents more than Odenathus. Whose access to her bed she restricts to the days when she knows herself to be fertile, according to the moon. Banishing him from her bed as soon as she has conceived.

It is fortunate for the royal relationship that Odenathus shares his wife's love of chivalry, & she his ambition to conquer the nearby empires of the Orient.

Together they wage a war against the Persian king, Sapor. But it is Zenobia who lays siege to his city. Who captures the Persian king with his great treasures & many concubines.

Immediately after the victory the pleasing Odenathus is mysteriously assassinated in his sleep. According to history: by jealous plotting relatives.

Who go undiscovered. & unpunished. & don't resurface — their murderous jealousies mysteriously appeased— when Queen Zenobia slips onto the vacated throne, & assumes unshared rulership over the aggrandized kingdom of Palmyra. —After resuming the unshared privacy of her body, as a widow.—

Awing the world with the wisdom & discipline of her reign, as she keeps adding to her kingdom. Her armies are stationed in Asia Minor, Syria, Mesopotamia, & Egypt.

When Aurelian becomes emperor of Rome she openly defies

him. But he defeats her: her first & final defeat. In 272 Palmyra falls. Queen Zenobia is captured & paraded through the streets of Rome, the highpoint of Aurelian's triumph.

But the world's respect for her is so great that the Romans give her an estate where she is allowed to live out the remainder of her virtuous life.

Virtue: from vir = man

A DIVINE ADVENTURE
HELENA PETROVNA BLAVATSKY, NÉE HAHN

July 30/31, 1831 (according to the Russian Calendar; at midnight: according to herself) or August 12,1831 (according to the Western Calendar; either way she is a path of life #7: the Number of Religious Quest) —May 8, 1891 As dictated by Madame (HPB) to Ursule Molinaro

The prodigal son is welcomed back into the fold with open arms. He has ploughed the lower depths of experience, & his return is a choice of "good" over "evil," made conscious by repentance. The fold rejoices: at this validation of its righteous ways.

But what about the prodigal daughter. Who repents of a stormy youth. Which the fold readily absolves if not applauds in the case of middle-aging prodigal sons. Who are expected to have sown wild oats. But which becomes a lurid past 25 vagabond years, tirelessly disinterred by contemporary journalists & subsequent biographers in the case of the middle-aging prodigal daughter.

Who does more than return to the fold. Who spends her conscious middle-aging life trying to restore the fold. To its original wisdom. To break down barriers   of creed/caste/race   that have obscured the fold's original wisdom. Which has become lost in particulars. In dogmas, that took up swords to enforce their particular interpretations of the obscured original wisdom.

Which the prodigal daughter tries to excavate from under garbage of history. Of centuries of power play. Growing shapeless   a giant tent of flesh; with unchangingly beautiful "azure" eyes, & unchangingly slender hands, ceaselessly rolling cigarettes   as she works immobilized at her desk, taking down dictations from Tibetan masters. Who dwell in her head.

Who call her: "Upasika"; sometimes: "the Old Woman."

& don't always express themselves clearly. Mixing messages of truth with metaphor, & wayward quotations, like other messengers of truth before them.

Before the prodigal dictation-taking daughter. Who is reproached for writing streams of unconsciousness. Fraudulently contrived mumbo-jumbo, that mentions   invents   a lost secret sacerdotal language: Senzar, which philologists cannot trace.

Which sweeps the credulous off their feet. Men & women of different creeds/castes/races. Who are often learned men & women. Often respectable; often from aristocratic backgrounds   —like the prodigal daughter herself.

They travel from all parts of the world to sit at the feet of the prodigal daughter.

Who is accused of hypnotizing her credulous followers with her unchangingly beautiful "azure" eyes. & of "having a way with men." & of sleight of hand, when she duplicates a sapphire ring she is wearing, or a heavy topaz, making an identical ring materialize in one outstretched unchangingly beautiful, cigarette-rolling hand. Or when she makes a message from one of the Tibetan masters drop on the balding head of an as-yet-skeptical newcomer.

Which she feels compelled to do because: Miracles are the

manure that makes religions grow. & a manifested ring or miracle letter is more convincing than the abstract teachings of occult sciences.

Which the world is not prepared to understand.

Which the prodigal daughter feels compelled to transmit. Considering herself a resuscitator rather than the inventor, as she works on her mission: to open the doors to the East, with the patience & perseverance that are essential for the study of occultism.

Of which phenomena are only incidental by-products.

Which the prodigal daughter produces. Prolifically. For which she is branded a fraud. The greatest impostor of the 19th century   of all centuries; of all times   by contemporary journalists & susbsequent biographers. Whose truths consist of dates & places.

Especially the dates & places relating to the prodigal daughter's   lurid   past. Beginning with her birth.

Which she is accused of mythologizing: As having occurred on the stroke of midnight. Making her proclaimed mission   —as the resuscitator of obscured wisdom; by opening the doors to the East—   look foreshadowed by the hour of her birth. Which looks like an attempt to re-tailor her past to suit her phenomenal present, to a skeptical biographer.

Who refuses to be taken in by mystery.

By mystification. Unnecessary mystification, which neglects to acknowledge a relationship between the prodigal daughter & her   once-famous   mother.   —The Russian novelist, pen-named: Zenaïda R——, who died, famous, at the age of 28.—

Whose memory the prodigal daughter allegedly shrouds in mists of early childhood. Too early to remember any mother-daughter relationship. Although the prodigal daughter is a biographical 12, at the death of her then famous mother.

Whose alleged deathbed concern about the future of her 12-year-old daughter is allegedly caused by the daughter's psychic powers.

An early manifestation of which allegedly drives a young serf to his death, after he allegedly displeases the then 5-or-6-year-old daughter. Who stares at him sternly, informing him that, by displeasing her he has displeased certain spirits. Who will avenge her by tickling him to death. Which allegedly sends the terrified boy running blindly across the snow, & into a river, where he drowns.

According to a skeptical posthumous biographer. Who unskeptically uses the childhood demonstration of psychic powers to explain away the adult prodigal daughter's impact on so many of her learned/respectable/aristocratic contemporaries. Who believe in the prodigal daughter's mission: as the resuscitator of obscured wisdom, who is opening the doors of the East.

Which posthumously disturbs many of her skeptical biographers. Whose biographical mission seems to be to "debunk" the mission of the prodigal daughter. In order to avenge credulous humanity. For its belief in miracles & supernatural dictations   —other than Christ's changing water into wine, or the Ten Commandments—   transmitted by an increasingly obese, chain-smoking woman.

Who allegedly waits to turn 50 to "come of age." & write & publish *Isis Unveiled,* & *The Secret Doctrine.* & endless articles.

Aging rapidly. For want of exercise. Indulging in biographical appetites of the flesh.

Including drugs: hashish, which she allegedly learns to smoke in Egypt. In the course of her meandering   lurid   past.

Which allegedly includes polygamy. & the birth of a crippled son, who dies in the course of perpetual travels, at the age of 5. & telling fortunes to her room neighbors in the community house for working women, where she first stays when she arrives   penniless   in New York City. Until she becomes famous.

Notorious: to most of her many posthumous biographers. Of all sexes. Whose conjectures & belittling insinuations will be punished into the 7th reincarnation. Like all sins; anybody's sin:

according to what the prodigal daughter has been told by her Tibetan masters.

Who send letters through her to the more adept of her believers, as she moves to India. & to various European towns. & finally to London, where she dies   not quite 60 years old   on May 8 (Eastern White Lotus Day), 1891, after rolling a last cigarette, which she hands to her doctor.

CHECKING
IN & OUT
OF HELL
JOAN
OF ARC

1412(?)– Wednesday, May 30, 1431

Have you been roasting in hell, Pierre Cauchon, Bishop of Beauvais. On a spit, like the pigs you used to feast on. Which your name recalls phonetically. (You become what you eat.)

Like my 19-year-old body, which you condemned to burn alive, on Wednesday, May 30, 1431. At the stake you'd had erected in the Old Market Place in Rouen.

Making my cry: Rouen, Rouen, are you to be my home! echo through history. Decrying your verdict: That I must burn alive for wearing clothes reserved for men   my armor   which looked to you like certain proof of devilish indecency on the body of a young woman. Proof of my heresy: Confirming your suspicion that I was hearing voice imitations done by the devil, not the commands of saints   —St. Michael, St. Catherine, St. Margaret, & St. Gabriel—   who had selected me, their Maid, to: drive the British out of France.

I promised that I'd change my armor for the womanly dress

you urged upon me, if you would let me go. Home to my mother, in my village in Domrémy.

Then pleaded with you: to cut off my head. Which I would suffer seven times rather than burning.

& cried: Bishop, I die through you! when you refused.

Were you transferred to hell, Pierre Cauchon, Bishop of Beauvais, when the church you'd represented sanctified the unwomanly young woman you'd burned for heresy, to make amends for your   & its   489-year-old mistake.

Which became your mistake alone, your iniquitous verdict.

Or sooner, on the second Sunday in May 1919, which the repentant history of France decreed to be my "Day," from that day on.

Or sooner still, in 1909, when your repentant church beatified the memory of the heretical unwomanly young woman whose life you had curtailed by burning.

Or way before then, back in 1456, 14 years after you yourself had died   —allowing you 14 years among the righteous— when eye witnesses of the trial over which you had presided rehabilitated the memory of my life & deeds.

When history & your church revised your judgment: from heretic to heroine.

Or were you plunged into an inner hell as soon as you watched the temporary flames die down around my charred remains, when you overheard the British   —whom you thought you were pleasing with your verdict—   wonder aloud if they: had burned a saint . . .

Which they had. Without a doubt. Any body sentenced to burn alive is sanctified by the sheer impact of the pain inflicted.

Besides, fire is known to purify. Was that not how you reasoned, Pierre Cauchon, Bishop of Beauvais, assuring me that you were saving my bedeviled soul from hell's eternal flames by sentencing my 19-year-old virgin body to the much briefer hell of temporary burning.

You were a leading churchman of our time, an erudite logician familiar with the history of ancient Greece, the basis of your careful education, where early gods issued direct commands to their obedient, until progressive thinking invented man's free will   — & woman's subjugation—   & the disgusted gods withdrew to wash their hands.

& you had read all the accounts of early Christian martyrs who had, like me, received divine commands that sent them on their often deadly missions. Curtailed, as mine was, by just as erudite, established judges.

Accounts which should have made you wonder about the blindness if not the insanity of those who'd caused such loss of saintly lives. Yet, you felt just as righteous as those early blinded madmen when you tortured an armored 19-year-old farmer's daughter into becoming yet another future saint.

Did you really believe that I had orders from the devil: "To drive the British out of France"?

(Which took my good King Charles (VII) twenty-two years to accomplish, until 1453, when only Calais remained in British hands, after my unwomanly example, topped by my public burning at your orders, stirred him to action.   Amending history's epitaph for him from: CHARLES THE INDOLENT to CHARLES THE VICTORIOUS.)

& did you think that I was going to accomplish the devil's mission, & did you fear for your British friends & friendships if you consented to my plea: To let me go home to my mother. & live a woman's life, drowning all echoes of my feats in village smallness.

Instead of causing me to suffer the rigorous education of your trial. Which subjected my simple farmgirl mind to the fierce juxtaposition of solitude & multitude, as I shuttled back & forth between your courtroom & my cell.

Which taught my simple farmgirl mouth to answer you "with clarity, simplicity, & skill." Which so impressed all those who heard my useless self-defense   —"It was wonderful to hear her speak"—   that they came forth to rehabilitate my memory   & demote yours   25 years later.

You need not have incurred your soul's damnation, Pierre Cauchon, Bishop of Beauvais   —nor history's & your church's amended judgment of you as: the iniquitous judge—   had you returned me home.

Not to my mother, but to my father. A righteous man much like yourself, justly concerned with his standing in the community.

He'd had recurrent dreams about me: His teenage daughter slipping on man's clothes, & running off with soldiers. It so upset him that he ordered my mother & my brothers to keep me in the house, occupied with sewing & spinning, instead of tending outdoor flocks.

Rather than witness the disgrace of his dream come true, my father had ordered my brothers to drown me if they caught me changing into pants. & if they refused he'd sworn to do the job himself.

I'm sure my father would have killed me somehow, if you had sent me home. He'd be roasting in hell instead of you, for all eternity. Justly concerned about his posthumous standing in the community. My unwomanly life was doomed to be brief.

Perhaps it was predestined, like the lives of the ancients, who'd also heard & heeded divine commands.

Who also became the subjects of much poetry & art. & passionate research. & history's repentance & revisions.

If you're remembered, Pierre Cauchon, Bishop of Beauvais, it is because of me. I am a saint now, so I'll let you share in the homage offered me by a Rouen restaurant in the Old Market Place that calls itself: Au Bûcher. (At the Stake.)

A SQUIRREL
FOR LOVE
CARO(LINE)
LAMB,
VISCOUNTESS
OF
MELBOURNE

November 13, 1785–
January 24, 1828

I was called slight all my life. Which did not offend me while I was a dark-eyed, golden-haired elf. Whom the family doctors diagnosed as: too slight to be subjected to learning. Anything at all.

My parents sent me to Italy instead. & later, when I was 9, to the house of my beautiful aunt, the Duchess of Devonshire, where I grew up with solid, placid cousins. Who called me Ariel, because I continued to be ethereally slight, or Squirrel, because I never sat still.

Obviously, somewhere between running & jumping & dancing & playing I learned how to read & write, or I couldn't have become the prominent Victorian novelist I was destined to become. Driven to writing by the agony of passion.

Besides, being illiterate would have been unthinkable for the daughter of an earl. Even a slight, highly high-strung daughter of an earl. I just didn't receive the formal education my sturdy cousins received. But I never felt slighted by the lack of it. I still thought of slight as slender & frail. Something desirable to be for an elf who was rapidly growing into a much courted young woman.

I began to resent the word only after I turned 16. When my slightness was blamed when I allegedly "collapsed in hysterics" during the ceremony that wed me to the aging Lamb   a man of 26 at the time, but aging to my 16-year-old eyes   who was to be my on-again/off-again husband for the next 19-20 years.

Whose ovine family considered me too slight to be a worthy ewe. Harmful to the political image of Queen Victoria's prime minister & advisor.

From the first day of our marriage they worked at poisoning his desire for me.

Which seemed to grow stronger with every new lover I took. & culminated when I fell incurably in love with "mad, bad, dangerous-to-know" Byron.

Who hurt me more than any man, woman, family, or family doctor had hurt me   —so deeply that I tried to kill myself— when he shrugged me off as just another one of his many SLIGHT infatuations.

Of course I would not let him shrug me off. & pursued him with years of threats, alternating with abject supplications. I even laid siege to his residence, until my aging Lamb arrived on the scene of scenes & made me go back home with him.

It was then that the ovine family tried to have me declared insane. When I was saner than ever. When I had just exposed all that Byron had done   —not only to me—   in my first just published novel *Glenarvon*. Which everyone was reading.

—All my books were published anonymously, but all my readers knew who had written them, anyway.—

A while before that I had also given birth to a child who had been declared an idiot, by the ovine family doctors. & the ovine family was hoping to prove the same of me, to obtain a legal separation for the father of the idiot child. But my aging Lamb didn't want to let go of me.

Ironically   or rather: predictably, as I understood later he waited for Byron to die, to leave me.

Byron's funeral procession happened to pass by my house. & I happened to see it. The thought that I had perhaps contributed to what some people called: his persecution, when I exposed him in my best-selling roman à clef   to avenge his slighting of my passion for him   shocked me into a frenzy of drugs & sex, to obliterate my guilt.

Obliterating mainly my aging Lamb's faithful desire for me. He gave in to almost 20 years of ovine family pressures, & ended as many years of marriage.

But he was a good Lamb, & he let me go on living in our country house in Brocket, which he knew I loved. He'd occasionally come to visit me there, but we never lived together again.

SLIGHT. Now that I am totally weightless   now that the satin flesh & porcelain bones of the Victorian novelist I allegedly typified have dissolved into the substance of clouds   the word echoes only offense. It is still used to describe my novels & my poetry. "As a writer she was slight." Dismissing any understanding reached through the impassioned pain of my characters' highly sensitive nervous systems as "a blend of [a] cuteness & frenzy."

A STAYED
LIFE
FRIDA
KAHLO

1919–1954   A sick city pigeon lies dying in the gutter, frightened of discovery. Gulls screech down on an injured gull & hack it to death. A hit stray dog flees howling down Mexican streets, pursued by stray dogs that overtake it   attack it   kill it. Killing the sickness/the injury/the dysfunction. But the human species organizes special Olympics for its handicapped, because the human species takes pride in telling nature: & yet . . . despite you . . . nonetheless.

The handicap as incentive.

She was not born handicapped. But she knew about handicaps from her father, a photographer from Hungary, whom she admired for continuing his work despite the threat of epileptic seizures that overshadowed his life.

& she'd felt singled out from birth by the thick single eyebrow that ran from temple to temple uninterrupted across the bridge of her nose, like a dark-furred frown. Adding a line of finality to the blunt square forehead. A signature of fate which she tried to decode in her mirror. In self-portraits of the: Mono-Brow, as she called herself. & painted   over & over   with the pride of "otherness." Of the chosen: portraying singularity as superiority.

As: stronger than, after the accident that broke her spine.

That incarcerated her passionate body in an unyielding corset. To hold it up. To make it stand   sit, as she grew weaker   in front of her easel.

Would Frida Kahlo have painted as passionately as much without the accident that handicapped her body.

That prevented her body from bearing the child she craved. Might not have craved as passionately, had she not become handicapped. Might not have painted so desperately: the plight of the doomed fetus desperately trying for a *buen exito,* a successful entry into life, had she not been handicapped.

Becoming a better painter than her better-known painter-husband Diego Rivera, in the opinion of some of their contemporaries. & in the increasingly numerous opinions of posthumous admirers/art critics/collectors.

& would Diego Rivera have tolerated a painter-wife who threatened to outpaint him

—Who portrayed him in miniature; across her mighty mono-brow   simultaneously portraying her jealous possessiveness of him in which he felt incarcerated like her torso in the unyielding corset—

had she not been handicapped.

But intact. A healthy   but perhaps equally possessive   mono-brow. Equally suspicious of every woman who stepped near their married circle. Whom the handicapped Frida suspected of trying to sneak her Diego to able-bodied adulterous freedom   —his natural habitat—   behind his jailer's corseted back.

Which she concealed in long peasant-embroidered dresses, in memory of her epileptic father's Hungarian past. Calling on the past to shield the present.

From female trespassers who resembled her neither in talent nor in   faulty   body. Or worse: who had a talent, with arrogant unbroken spines. Who lingered on the periphery of the married circle   —of the "unholy alliance," as some of them called it—   under pretexts of sharing political passions. Until she schemed or screamed them away.

Scheme-screaming herself into a divorce, eventually.

Which she painted. Over & over. Pride-portraits of her misery. Of the mistake. The error of their separation. Their separate lonelinesses. Drawing him back into a second married circle, with the magnet of her passionate talent, her talented passion. A second unholy alliance, as stormy as the first. That reincarcerated both in the possessive corset of her jealousy.

Which grew at the deterioration rate of her spine. Until she could no longer stand upright. & painted sitting, in her house in Coyoacan which has become the museum of her life.

In her place on the bed in the bedroom lies the unyielding corset, covered with the flowers she painted on its stiff plaster whiteness.

THE
APOLLONIAN
AGE:
A DEMOTION
FOR THINKING
WOMEN

CASSANDRA

ca. 1200 B.C.   Cassandra writes a letter to Apollo:

Most Fair Unfair Apollo—
Perhaps it will flatter Your Godship to receive in Your retirement
the appeal of a humble mortal who has long ceased to be, yet
cannot rest in peace.

Injustice has an independent life & does not always die together
with its victims. Who die in flesh alone, fed on resentment.

You made a ghost of me that lives inside all women born since
my time. Whose plight began with mine. You set a precedent
when You spat upon my right to turn You down.

The men who saw You spit, & watched my punished life, began
to chuckle, rubbing hands that itched with ownership. They fan-
cied they were little gods, mortal Apollos, who timed the loving
of their women & made mothers out of mates. Chattel, whose hair
was worth more than their brains.

Now that predestined fate has given way to self-determination, & meddling in the lives of men no longer is Your Godship's duty   —or prerogative—   You may at long last find the time to hear the plaint of Cassandra, Princess & Prophetess of Troy.

Perhaps Your present ineffective state has made Your Godship ponder the causes of effects. & unless lingering memories of grandeur obstruct Your logic, You may have sought the cause of Your undoing in something You once did. & may have found the seed of Your demotion in Your saliva in my mouth.

I saw Your fall   the fall of all Greek gods   in the lightning flash of Clytemnestra's ax upon my throat, & knew that Your injustice would be justly paid.

Still, Your demise does not mean my redemption. I could forgive You, & redeem myself. But Your saliva has congealed into a cud between my teeth. & between the teeth of all the women born after me. Who have been ruminating the right that You denied me. A woman's right to give or to withhold her body.

Which mortal men in turn denied them. Making a law of Your example, that forces women to spread submissive compass legs at a pressure of their thumbs.

If I forgave You   myself   my worried mother's coaxing counsel to let You have that fatal kiss . . . One kiss, at least, Cassandra, daughter, He's after all a god . . . & even Clytemnestra who was as much as I a marionette of fate   I'd be anachronistic, a pagan B.C. saint.

I'd also set a classical example for women still alive today to let themselves be spat upon by slowly shrinking fading gods. Who will become as ineffective & as ornamental as You've become, unless I am redeemed by Your repentance.

In Greek, the word repentance means: a change of mind.

Changing Your mind can change if not the life You made me live, at least the legend that I left behind.

Posthumous reputation is still unfair to me.

You'll say that woman's vanity lives on though she be dead. But Your changed mind will realize that other women live, & may believe in You again, if you dispel the disbelief that met my truth. & still meets theirs. Your exile has the confines of my myth.

Your Godship cannot make a comeback unless You first correct the image my name projects in modern minds. Where I'm made out to look like the gloom & doom which I predicted: A madwoman, old before her years. Wild-eyed & sallow-skinned; one bony arm raised like a scream. & all around me, exasperated shrugging Trojans muffle their ears with their hands, not to hear my ugly strident voice.   —Some even blame the fall of Troy on me.—   While You, the instigator of it all, continue to evoke untarnished beauty. & intelligence.

I realize that messengers grow to resemble the news they bring. & are given little credit for telling the truth. But You know as well as I that I was beautiful. Had I been plain, Your Godship would have devised some other means than courting me to make my knowledge worthless.

Forgive me. It's tedious to be reminded of a dead desire; that was, moreover, unrequited. Perhaps, had I been plain, a God's attentions might have flattered me into submission. But I was as golden & lovely as Homer says I was. With a voice as sweet as a songbird's.

But Homer   blind & lyrical   fails to mention my prophetic gift. Nowhere does he acknowledge the fact that I foretold the story he recorded. That I foresaw the long drag of the siege. Every boring detail of the heroic slaughter.

I recognized Paris as my brother before Paris himself knew who he was.

Homer was writing five centuries after the fall, when knowledge had become unbecoming, for a woman.

He could not let intelligence & beauty share the same female face, if he desired to be read.

He thought that he was being kinder to my memory, making me beautiful rather than wise.

But without my knowledge I become unimportant. & banal. Just another beautiful princess who walked the streets of Troy. A minor Helen.

Poor Helen. Legend has made of her the sample type of the new woman that came about with male supremacy. Placidly beautiful, without a mind of her own. Open to the windy choice of men. Of any man, as long as she was loved. & kept. She has become the classic femme fatale with whose defenseless image modern Helenist pigs still play their ever-adolescent games of solitaire.

I had decided to defy Your strategy of competition among women. To be a friend to Helen when Paris brought her into Troy. It was an easy task. Helen was excellent company, soothing & bright, a smiling moon.

I never envied her. Not even when I foresaw her enviable ample end, drugged & immortalized, still worshipped by posterity. & the bloody horror of mine. Perhaps hers was a wisdom that I could not share. Because I saw too much. Or not enough.

How could I blame her for her fate? I'd read the signs & understood that You would use the war against my city to denigrate the female side of life. By severing woman's charm from woman's mind. Repainting owl-wise Athena as an old maid.

Did You resent the minds of those who had withstood Your court-ship? Who saw as I had seen the power greed behind the sunshine halo of Your smile?

& all the others whom You raped & metamorphosed, yet could not integrate into Your maleness.

Your Godship's unfulfilled ambitions streamed together like a flood, at Thetis's wedding party. When Eris —uninvited— tossed the contentious apple "to the Fairest." At Your behest?

& was Zeus heeding Your advice when He decided that a mortal be the judge & dispatched Hermes down to Paris to have my estranged brother make the loaded choice He would not make Himself: between His wife, His daughters, & His dreams?

You saw Your chance of added power, watching the losers' rivalry unleash a war against my city.   —Whose walls Your Godship feigned to be defending while in Odysseus' fertile mind You sowed the horse-shaped ruse.

You chuckled at the thought of being worshipped more than Zeus   as the great god of new civilizations   by men whom You'd make rulers of the roost, after You banished womankind from life's decisions.

Your war against a woman's right to think, so deviously set up, it looked to all concerned as though a woman were the cause of man's disaster.

I clearly saw the fall of women once the walls of Troy came down.

Ironically, Your Godship fell soon after.

Or perhaps not so ironically. Perhaps You overtipped the scale when You enslaved half of humanity, & passed a law against female intelligence.

Matter weighs more heavily than mind: it pulled You down.

An alien principle took charge when men began administering nature. When priestesses whose moon-based calendar foretold the cycles with minute precision gave way to priests in women's robes who reckoned by the sun, & left each year awry with one fourth of a useless day.

All forms of life will choke, on earth, leaving no vestige of the Great Apollo, unless You render unto women the right to think & speak their minds   & to be heard   of which You robbed us all the day You spat into my mouth.

Eternally,

κασσάηϑρα

P.S. There always seems to be an apple   & a woman; & a snake   at the beginning of the end. Apollo, after all, means: Appleman. & in Your temples bred the all-knowing whispering sacred serpents.

KNITTING
BROWS
AROUND THE
GUILLOTINE
OLYMPE DE
GOUGES

1745(?)/1748(?)/ 1755(?)–November 3, 1793

According to Lord Raglan better known for the cut of his sleeves than for his theories on heroism a birth shrouded in mystery is one of the basic ingredients for the making of a hero.

On this premise alone Olympe de Gouges amply qualifies:

1. Records of her age disagree by a full decade. Did she lie, on the eve of her execution, when she told her judges that she was 38? A church record gives the date of her baptism as May 7, 1745, which would suggest that she was 48 instead. On her last night in jail she allegedly admitted to being 40, even 41, to fellow cellmates who cattily filtered the correction to encyclopedists waiting in the wings of history.

2. No one seems to have known the name of her father, whom rumors randomly select among prominent noblemen, all the way up the courtly ladder to Louis XV.

3. & perhaps she intentionally contributed to the myth that continued to shroud her adult person by claiming early widowhood   —predating it, perhaps, after one year of marriage to a rich & elderly Parisian known only as: Monsieur Aubry; after the birth of a son—   to reclaim the freedom to take lovers. & to write.

Undisputed facts of her life are:

1. That she was born in Montauban, Southern France.
2. That her mother was a wardrobe mistress, known for wit, beauty, & lovers.
3. That she herself was beautiful   —flawless Mediterranean skin, charcoal eyes, a dusky cloud of hair. Acknowledged even by the men who opposed her urgent pleas for women's participation in political decisions. Who ridiculed the style in which she wrote her message-plays/poetry/political tracts. An Oriental novel: *The Philosopher Prince.* & called her passion for justice a platform for female vanity & pride.
4. That she founded the Club of the *Tricoteuses,* symbols of female sobriety & thrift, who sat knitting around the guillotine, midwifing the bloody birth of Freedom, Equality, & Sisterhood. Until they eventually degenerated, along with the principles of the Revolution, & became the strident hyenas depicted in history books.
5. That, in 1791, she drew up THE DECLARATION OF THE RIGHTS OF WOMEN AS CITIZENS. In which she stipulated that all official positions should be open to both sexes, based solely on character & qualification.   —In Article 10 she states: "If women have the right to mount the scaffold, they must also have the right to mount the political platform." A self-prophetic sentence for which she is remembered as a French national heroine. Almost two centuries of French schoolchildren have been learning it by heart, although, during the two years that followed its publication, the militantly anti-feminist *Convention* suppressed all the rights she

had proclaimed. & even persuaded her son Pierre Aubry to testify against her.

6. That she was executed on November 3, 1793. By then, Louis XVI   (possibly the son of her half-brother, if her father had really been Louis XV?)   had been tried for treason to his people, & decapitated. Shocking her into abandoning the Revolution. & even the feminist cause. She attacked Robespierre for betraying his & her   initial ideals, & suggested that they drown themselves together. He to expiate regicide, & she to mourn the future of women.

Perhaps she deliberately courted the guillotine, because her disappointment in the Revolution was too desperate to wish to survive the brief promise of sexual equality to which she had dedicated her life.

Sacrificing one's life to a principle or an ideal is another ingredient for heroism, although Lord Raglan did not think of women as potential candidates. He was 5 when Olympe de Gouges lost her head, & by the time he was old enough to write down his theories women were once again knitting exclusively inside the home.

TRADING TABOOS

KA'AHUMANU, QUEEN & FIRST CO-RULER OF HAWAII

March 17, 1765,*
to June 5, 1832

She is 6 feet tall, & weighs 300 lbs. A proof of noble birth among the people of her islands, who measure majesty by their trees.

& she is a champion surfer, fear-taught as a small girl when she's swept out to sea, away from the coast of Maui, the Valley Island on which she was born. For hours she flails & paddles. Finally she catches a wave that rides her back to shore.

Catching the right moment seems to become her pattern, as she grows up. & is given in marriage to King Kamehameha I. The Great. The Lonely Warrior. A Hawaiian Napoleon who united the separate islands under his single crown, in 1810.

Who allegedly had 21 wives.

He is aging when the majestic 13-year-old becomes his favorite

---

* March 17, 1765, is celebrated as her birthday by the society that bears her name. Historical accounts don't give a day, & the year is placed anywhere between 1765 & 1777.

wife. Second in rank only to his "sacred" wife. Keopuolani, the mother of the heir to his throne.

The 2 high-ranking queens are not jealous of each other. They're still living by premissionary morals, which accept polygamy as one of the economic privileges of upper-class men & women.

But the aging Kamehameha is incensed when his new teenage wife tries to do as he has done, 21 alleged times over. When she casts an acquisitive eye upon a young chief at the court.

His rage drives her back to her family on Maui. Where she holds out until a British navigator & friend of the king comes to plead with her to return to her royal husband. Whose public image as the victorious warrior cannot bear giving in to a woman.

After their reconciliation Kamehameha says of her: "She is all things. & she is undefeatable. Strong in times of crises, she also rides the waves like a bird. & she is as lovely as a lauhala blossom."

He loves & respects her so deeply that he creates a government post for her, as his *Kuhina nui*, his co-ruler & official equal. — Perhaps he also hopes to rivet her attention on matters of state, away from other young chiefs at the court.— The new office gives Ka'ahumanu the right to veto any of the king's decisions, & to make counterproposals. To which he listens. Her opinions are often shrewder than his own; he encourages her to be outspoken.

But she does not speak out to him about how humiliated she feels when she must avert her female face every time she passes a holy place, if she does not wish to face death at the hands of the priests.

Not once in the years they rule together does she complain to him about the daily indignity that separates them at mealtimes. Of the taboo that forbids women to eat in the company of men. To eat the same foods as the men.

Who have always done the cooking on the islands. & may have created the taboos, the *kapus*, in order to reserve the better foods for themselves: coconuts   bananas   pork   the fleshier types of fish   the most coveted delicacy: baked dog. Which are all forbidden to women.

Men were also the priests on the islands. Who carried out the orders & enforced the punishments of the gods.   —& removed the right eyeball of a 5-year-old girl   mercifully, instead of killing her, since she was only 5 years old   in divine retaliation for having eaten a banana.

It is only after Kamehameha I dies   on May 8, 1819   that Ka'ahumanu begins a subtle campaign to abolish the eating taboos.

During periods of mourning all taboos were suspended. Men & women ate together   & of the same foods   while they mourned together. Wailing loudly. Often disfiguring themselves permanently   —burning semi-circles into their cheeks, or knocking their front teeth out with rocks—   in demonstration of their grief over the death of their great king.

Whose royal flesh was steamed off the dismembered corpse, & offered to the sea. & whose royal bones were wrapped in black tapa cloth   made of beaten tree bark   & placed in a basket braided of wild mountain vines. Which 2 retainers carried to a secret burial place at a distant location known only to them.

Before Liholiho ascends the throne, on May 29, 1819, to rule as Kamehameha II, he is confronted by Ka'ahumanu. She is wearing his dead father's long feather cloak & helmet. Symbols of rulership & power   —which led to the extinction of many types of island birds—   never before worn by a woman. "You & I are to share the kingdom. Such was the will of your father," she tells him.

The new king acquiesces. He is used to obeying the will of his father. & the will of his father's favorite wife & co-ruler. Who will now become *his* co-ruler.

He is also used to deferring to his mother, Keopuolani, from when he was a small boy, when she'd made him submit to daily head massages that were to give him a nobler, more elongated head.

& he has become used to the sight of women eating men's food in the presence of men, during the mourning period that followed his father's death & funeral. But when his widowed mother begins to eat a banana in front of him, offered to her by Ka'ahumanu, he averts his face & quickly walks away. He does not wish to become implicated in the divine punishment that must befall his mother if the *kapus* are the commands of the gods, as the priests have taught him to believe all his life.

Although he has watched the foreigners who have recently come to the islands break all sorts of taboos, & nothing evil has seemed to happen to them. But the foreigners are all men. They did not bring their women with them. Instead they brought the strong drink which Liholiho has tasted. & likes.

He is confused. & Ka'ahumanu gives him no peace. Every day she speaks to him about the hardships the separate food preparations & eating arrangements place not only on the women, but also on the cooking men. Affirming   against the affirmations of the priests, who also give their new king no peace   that nothing bad will happen if men & women continue eating together, as during the recent mourning period. That his   & her subjects will thank him, that he'll be remembered with gratitude by generations to come, if he abolishes the eating taboos.

Which she urges him to do at once, by eating at the women's table, publicly, during a banquet she is planning to give, with her ally, his mother Keopuolani.

Who continues to eat bananas behind his hastily turned back. & in front of his round-eyed younger brother Kauikeaouli.

The banquet takes place in October 1819. There is a blatantly empty space at the women's table, between Ka'ahumanu & his mother. Bravely the new king walks over to it, followed by the eyes of all the guests. He is so embarrassed that he stuffs into his mouth whatever his hands encounter on the table. Expressing exaggerated delight at the taste of women food to an audience of aghast men & women; & pensive priests. Who have all stopped eating, & are watching their new king's throat, as he swallows bite after bite, without divine interference.

The high priest thinks that he is watching his religion disappear down the king's throat.

He is not surprised when Ka'ahumanu gives orders to burn all holy places & images, in November 1819. Or when she organizes women into military units, in foresighted preparation for the revolts by subjects in remote areas who still cling to the old gods & ways.

There is a brief civil war, which ends in the victory of the king's & Ka'ahumanu's army, & officially establishes free eating throughout the islands.

The first missionaries rejoice when they land, on March 30, 1820, & are told that the natives have burned all their "heathen" gods. But they rejoice too soon. "We just got rid of our old gods. We need no new ones," Ka'ahumanu tells the delegation of "mirthless men," when they finally come to see her to seek her permission to stay & work on the islands. After many permission-seeking visits to Liholiho. After they've finally been made aware of her co-ruling power position, which they had not expected a woman to hold, on the islands.

A woman who keeps a pet pig   a corpulent black boar that follows her wherever she goes. His will-fed stomach is the pillow on which she lays her head when she sleeps.

She barely acknowledges their presence, & holds out a disdainful little finger in sign of their dismissal. They have interrupted the card game she has learned to play from the other   non-missionary   foreigners.

Whose strong drink has become Liholiho's favorite indulgence. Which does not predispose him to listen to delegations of Calvinists in quest of sin.

Although he does eventually permit them to teach reading & writing   the *palapala*   to him. & to other members of the ruling class.   —Ka'ahumanu learns it in a week; Liholiho drops out.—   Who will decide whether or not reading & writing is good. Before deciding whether or not it should be taught to the rest of their people.

It takes Ka'ahumanu 4 years to change her mind about the missionaries. While she lets them teach her more & more complicated *palapala*. Which she enjoys. More than the other foreigners' card games.

& she watches them help the sick. Who have multiplied, especially among the poorer of her subjects, since the introduction of the other foreigners' strong drink. Of which she disapproves as much as the missionaries do. They agree that alcohol is an evil. A sin.

But they have trouble agreeing on the definition of adultery as another sin, when Ka'ahumanu abducts & marries the already married king of Kuai, on October 9, 1821. & shortly thereafter marries also the   still single   son of the king of Kuai. Scandalizing the missionaries when she comes driving to their church on Sundays, proudly displaying her 2 new husbands.

Gradually they persuade her to give up at least the son.   — Who is not exactly a faithful new husband. Which makes her as angry as she made Kamehameha I when she was his new teenage queen.

She has begun to listen to the missionaries. Whose preaching becomes more convincing as her majestic body becomes less reliable. Perhaps monogamy is a divine command, that intends for a woman & a man to grow old together. Like the missionaries, who brought their   long-necked   women with them, & seem to live with the same one all the time.

After Queen Keopuolani dies, & Liholiho travels to England with his favorite wife, in November 1823, to ask George IV to place the islands under British protection, Ka'ahumanu becomes sole regent.

—"Ruling her people with a rod of iron, during that transitional period that saw the residence of the first foreigners on the islands": according to one of those first foreigners.—

& when Liholiho's favorite wife dies of the measles in London, soon followed by the grief-stricken Liholiho himself, Ka'ahumanu remains sole regent. Even after Liholiho's younger brother Kaui-keaouli ascends the throne as Kamehameha III.

Early in 1824 she establishes the islands' first law code. It orders: Observance of the Sabbath, & learning *palapala*. & forbids: murder   fighting   theft   drinking alcohol   polygamy /adultery.   —Adulterers are condemned to forced labor. She has them build roads, the first on the islands. Surprising newly arrived foreigners with their number & intricacy.

& pleasing the missionaries. But not enough to baptize her when she asks them to be baptized, on April 19, 1824. Their turn has come to keep her waiting. Until December 5, 1825, when she becomes an official Christian, named: Elizabeth.

& such an ardent Calvinist that she opposes the landing of French Catholic missionaries, almost risking a diplomatic break with France. Eventually she compromises by allowing the French ship to land, but forbidding her subjects to attend Catholic mass.

For the last month of her life she is gravely ill, & forced to stay in bed, surrounded by her missionaries.

Who rush the first printed Hawaiian copy of the Bible to her deathbed. It is bound in red leather, with ELIZABETH engraved in gold. She reads her Christian name like an absolution, clutching the book to her heart as she dies.

On a picture by the British-born painter of Hawaiians, Madge Tennant: *Ka'ahumanu Sunning Herself,* the naked queen lies on her side, massive like one of her island mountains, fire turning liquid under the burnished-amber skin.

In her foothills, an ant of a European-looking man, elegant with hat & cane, stands gazing up.

THE
STAMINA OF
IMPERVIOUSNESS
LUCY
GOODALE
THURSTON

October 29, 1795–
October 13, 1876

May she go to college? the 16-year-old Lucy Goodale asks her father, a New England farmer & deacon. Fearfully. To her, he is a deputy of the Heavenly Father whose commandments regulate every word & gesture of her family's life.

His instant Yes surprises her. It's your life, he says, only you can fulfill it.

For a shocked moment she wonders: If he loves her as much as she has always assumed. How can he let her go so readily? But her doubt is promptly vanquished by guilt. & by the joyful anticipation of continued learning.

She graduates from Andover College, & becomes a schoolteacher.

In September 1819, one of her brothers arranges an introduction to one of his fellow graduates from Anderson Theological Seminary, a former scythemaker named Asa Thurston, who gave up his craft to become a missionary.

Asa Thurston wishes to sail for Hawaii   then known as: the Sandwich Islands   to spread Protestant Christianity among the natives. But the Board for Foreign Missions does not accept un-married missionaries. It funds only couples: $400 a year, plus $50 a year for each child. Asa Thurston is looking for a wife.

On the way to their first meeting, the brother transmits a ten-tative marriage proposal to Lucy. She takes it to her father, to tell her what she should tell Asa Thurston. Again her father's instant acquiescence: It is your life . . . etc. . . . . shocks her by his read-iness to let her go. To the end of the world, this time. She may never see him again. Or anyone she has known for these 24 years of her life. She is frail. He knows that she has dizzy spells, & sometimes coughs blood. In her head, a kaleidoscope starts ro-tating mosaics of fear, Christian adventure, & her father's dis-concerting detachment.

On October 12, 1819 she marries Asa Thurston. On October 23, 1819 they climb aboard the brig *Thaddeus*. "Bound for the land of darkness," she thinks. They become acquainted during the 5½ months of seasickness that finally ends on April 4, 1820, when they land at Kailua, the principal town on the   Big Island of Hawaii.

Where they'll spend the next 40 years of their lives.

That very day she begins the diary which she eventually com-piles into: *The Life and Times of Lucy G. Thurston*. It spans over half a century of native & missionary interaction, described by an increasingly wistful observer, who does not exclude herself from her sense of humor.

Who can't fall asleep on her first non-seasick night on land. In a begrudgingly assigned house. "Due to fleas, and native curi-osity." The islanders have never seen white women before, & trail Lucy wherever she goes. Even inside the house of her first rest. They keep touching her on arms, & breasts, & thighs with a probing finger, as though to find out if there's a body inside her ankle-length skirt & long-sleeved blouse, with its stiff, chin-high collar. That makes her: a Long-Neck, to the fact-seeking natives. &: a Non-Laugher, because of the grave white face that peers back at them, as they peer beneath her tightly tied bonnet.

They're everpresent. They watch her cook   —in shocked
surprise: all cooking is done by men, on the islands. They
see   & touch   her sweat, & ask why she keeps her body
covered in the hottest weather. She tries to convey to them that:
It's not decent for human beings to go around without clothes. &
leaves them thinking that she's perhaps obeying a taboo that requires sweating, & other bodily discomforts. Which makes them
feel sorry for her, since they recently freed themselves of their
own taboos. They can't understand how the uncomfortable Long-
Neck can feel equally sorry for them.

The more Lucy G. Thurston learns about the natives
—in their scanty wraps made of tree bark, which she watches
the women beat into tapa cloth "that can ill bear washing" . . .

Which is spread over ruling-class couples, to signify marriage,
between partners that "come together or separate at the dictates
of convenience and inclination . . ."

& dyed black, to wrap the bones of the ruling-class dead, after
the flesh has been steamed off & tossed into the sea . . . —

About the ruling-class women who go to a plateau strewn with
large, reddish-brown "birthing" stones, with rounded indenta-
tions of varying sizes, onto which they prop themselves to give
birth . . .

to babies that are placed into a dark pit where the sun can't
see them die, when the father is deemed too low-born to produce
a ruling-class child . . .

the more she feels that the land to which she has come is even
darker than her premonitions.   —Once a year her exile is interrupted by mail. A letter from Boston takes a year to reach her,
& another year for the writer to receive her reply.—   A land
whose godless inhabitants live from day to day, in spiritual &
physical insecurity. At the mercy of rulers who can dispossess
them of their house, & everything they own, upon an hour's
notice.

& that she must teach them continuity by example. & keep her
house open to them   —"Missionaries are public characters,

and their houses must be public houses."— so that they can learn responsibility from watching "Brother and Sister Thurston" live.

—On a photograph of "Brother and Sister Thurston" in their Kailua house, a plump, earnest middle-aged New England woman sits beside a gaunt Father Time, with a flowing white beard.—

The Thurstons are the only missionary family that does not send their children to boarding schools on the mainland. Lucy teaches her 3 daughters & 2 sons at home. But she makes sure that they're never exposed to any contact with the natives, & keeps them ignorant of the local language until they reach the age of 14. When she considers them sufficiently rooted in New England Calvinism to be immune to the seduction of thoughtless sunshine. At 14, they're permitted to learn Hawaiian, & to help her teach children of the ruling class how to read & write.

Despite the loneliness & isolation Lucy's lungs improve in the island climate. "Sickness is said to be a sin. I try to avoid it," she writes in her diary after she has a tumored breast removed in an anesthesia-less operation that lasts an hour & a half. She endures it sitting in an armchair, asking the surgeon before each cut how long it will take, & where exactly it will be, so that she can "make herself bear it."

When the initially sturdier Asa becomes partially paralyzed, they give up their house of 40 years, & move to Honolulu to be closer to medical care. She survives him by 8 years, spending most of her time compiling her memoirs.

To which she adds that: her exiled life has been well spent, because "Vice [has] fled from the open face of day to dens and secret places." The ruling class has begun to wear clothes, passing the fashion down to their subjects. The men now look like men in Britain, France, or America. & the women are walking around in the loose, ankle-long cotton gowns the missionaries gradually coaxed over their heads. They're calling their new dresses: mumus/sleepwear, because they'd first agreed to wear them at night, when it got chilly, when it made more sense to be wrapped up.

A New England traveler who visited the 75-year-old Lucy G. Thurston, a then recent & respected widow in Honolulu, was puzzled how "she had not lost one atom of the New England look."

A CIVIL

CIVIL WAR

BETSY

STOCKTON

ca. 1789–
October 24, 1865

The initial of her first name keeps recurring in chronicles of the white lives that looped with hers. The chronicled lives of professional Protestants, to whom she becomes: "Our faithful B——." An astonishingly capable assistant. The organizer of daring schools for the hitherto untaught. An unexpected scholar, coincidentally of the female sex. Barred from being thought of as a woman by the color of her skin. & by the white Protestants' concentration on their mission: To convert the heathen to the Christian faith.

Against which "B——" seems to have rebelled, at the beginning of her life.

She is recorded as an impious child, born into slavery of "unrecorded" parents. Who probably were slaves of the newborn's "owner," Robert Stockton. A last name that becomes affixed to her like the label on a steamer trunk.

Which is more or less how she is shipped off to Princeton, when she's in her early teens. When she is perhaps separated from her unrecorded parents   her unrecorded mother   who may or may not still be alive. Still the slave(s) of Robert Stockton. Who is sending the teenage slave girl to his married daughter, as a present.

To the discomfort of the married daughter's husband, the Reverend Ashbel Green, president of Princeton College. He does not wish to offend his father-in-law, but he fears for the faith of his growing sons, watching an impious teenage slave girl grow into an impious young slave woman.

Whom he finally arranges to have shipped off to another reverend. "To save her from the snares and temptations of the city" (of Princeton). "She showed no piety . . . or permanent seriousness throughout her adolescence," he writes, expressing the hope that she may have "a change of heart" under the beneficent influence of his esteemed colleague.

The suggested change of heart gradually takes place. Perhaps the astonishingly nimble mind of the coincidentally female young slave has discovered the advantages of least resistance. It greatly improves her position in the household of the other reverend master. Who deems that his beneficent influence has been sufficient, & ships her back to the Greens.

Her new eagerness to learn conquers Ashbel Green's earlier misgivings. She is allowed free access to the Green library, & the Green sons are allowed to help her with her studies, as she prepares to become an official Christian. After she is baptized in the Princeton Presbyterian Church the Greens officially give her her freedom, & place her in charge of their household.

But continuing to live with the family that knew her as a slave   & sent her away for 4 years for impious behavior   has a lingering aftertaste of being owned. She needs to go far away to leave her past behind. To become the owner of herself.

She asks to join a group of Protestant missionaries who are sailing for the Sandwich Islands. She is accepted as "assistant" to the Reverend Stewart & his family, on the written recommendation of her ex-owner, Mrs. Green. Whose letter stresses that her ex-slave is better "qualified for higher employment than domestic drudgery." That she is an exceptional scholar, "particularly versed in sacred history and mosaic institutions."

Besides being an excellent nurse. Which may have decided her acceptance: Mrs. Stewart is of delicate health.

In "a most unusual agreement," signed on November 18, 1822 by Betsy Stockton, the Reverend Stewart, & the Reverend Green, the Stewarts pledge to regard their assistant "neither as an equal nor as a servant . . . but as a humble Christian friend, embarked in the great enterprise of endeavoring to ameliorate the condition of the heathen."

After 6 months at sea the Stewarts & their humble Christian friend arrive at Lahaina, on the Island of Maui. Where they settle.

Betsy Stockton is probably the first black person to visit Hawaii. She very quickly learns the local language & opens the first school for "Commoners," which is attended by 30 farmer-students. She teaches them not so much the religion of her former masters   — who gave her her freedom—   as reading & writing, the initial tools of her own emancipation.

In his chronicle, the Reverend Stewart mentions her "fine school, in the chapel adjoining the yard," of the Stewarts, who have given her a wing of their house. She has become their "faithful B——," who runs their exiled household, raises their children, & nurses Mrs. Stewart, whose delicate health turns into severe illness.

It forces them to return to the mainland after only 2½ years. "Faithful B——" continues to raise the Stewart children, until several years after Mrs. Stewart's death, in 1830.

When her career as a founder & director of schools for the hitherto untaught seems to affirm itself. For a year she teaches toddlers in Philadelphia. Then organizes a school for Indians in Canada. & eventually she opens & directs what later becomes the "Witherspoon Street Colored School" in Princeton. Which she

runs until her death, on October 24, 1865.   —Less than 2
months before slavery is abolished in the United States, on December 18, 1865.

On a photograph, her grainy middle-aged profile stares into grainy
space.

HOMECOMING
TO A
FOREIGN
SHORE
MADGE
TENNENT

June 22, 1889–
February 5, 1972

Some northerners look down on any-body living beneath them on the map. & if their profession   or their curiosity   takes them to southern climates, they bottle their northernness & carry it with them for a continued feeling of hardy superiority.

While others trade their poorly heated overcast past for sunshine & tropical colors, which make them feel, like Madge Tennent, that they "live aesthetically" for the first time in their lives.

Madge Tennent was a northerner only by British birth & British complexion. Her exposure to the character-building influence of British weather lasted only through early childhood.   —It gave her asthma when she returned to London for an exhibit of her paintings in 1935.—   When she was five, her parents decided to move to South Africa.

They were unusual parents, with many interests & talents. Her father was an architect who often worked as a carpenter, & a painter of seascapes; her mother wrote, edited, cast astrological charts, held séances, & gave piano concerts. They thought it natural that their daughter started to draw seriously, & to paint, when she was 11, & a student at a Paris convent school.

Madge had always been tall for her age, & they had treated her like a grownup ever since she began traveling with them. She continued to travel with them through & beyond her adolescence, commuting between South Africa & Paris. Where she was briefly inspired to try her hand at fashion designing.

She was heading a government school for the arts in Johannesburg when she met   & soon married   Hugh Tennent, a "chartered" accountant from New Zealand. But their marriage was interrupted by WWI. He left to fight in France, while she & their first son went to live with his parents in New Zealand.

When he came back   with a severe injury to his right arm   the prospects of building an accounting firm in New Zealand looked gloomy. By now they had two sons to raise, & they thought they might do better in postwar England.

In 1923 they boarded a British freighter in Samoa, but when it docked in Hawaii   —briefly: to take on additional cargo— Madge Tennent got off the boat, & never got back on.

She felt that she had landed in the landscape of the paintings of Gauguin. Whom she admired more than any other painter. Whose remark: "Criticism passes, but good work remains," she quoted to herself every time a gallery rejected her bold, unwomanly style.

They cancelled the rest of their trip, & the whole family stayed in Gauguin's landscape.

Where she found a native culture "far more spiritual than the Calvinist missionaries." A culture of "Super Polynesians," with the "strength & grace of a sailing ship in full sail," who reminded her of ancient Greeks in their legends & bearing.

She longed to paint them, but for many years she drew & painted mainly the wives & children of "Caucasians" to support her family until her husband's firm got off the ground.

When she was finally able to paint her "true subjects"   — large-bodied Hawaiian women, elegant, graceful, & refined in their monumental size—   she sculpted them with a palette knife in a three-dimensional style she invented, & called: Rhythm in the Round.

"Through my life runs the story of remembered beauty—the sun-gilt bronze of a native," she says about them toward the end of her life.

The peripatetic northern child & young woman was 34 when she instantly recognized her aesthetic reality in Hawaii. She did not leave again, except to attend exhibits of her work in other places.   —To which she'd travel with bottled sunshine in her luggage, to protect her against the cold of critics.

A
CHRISTIAN
MARTYR IN
REVERSE

HYPATIA

A.D. 370–415   The screams of a 45-year-old Greek
philosopher being dismembered* by
early-5th-century Christians, in their early-5th-century church of
Caesareum, in Alexandria, center of early-5th-century civilization,
reverberated between the moon gate & the sun gate of that civilized
Egyptian city.

Before the philosopher's broken body was thrown into the civilized Alexandrian gutter, for public burning.

& smoke signals rose from the disorderly chunks of her charring
flesh, warning future centuries of reformers & healers that they
must hush their knowledge if they wished to avoid burning as
heretics, or witches. If they wished to stay alive.

In a world run by a new brand of Christians, politicians of
faith, who outlawed independent thought. Especially when
thought by women. Whom they offered a new role model   of
depleasurized submission   as they converted the great & lusty

---

*According to *The Women's Encyclopedia of Myths and Secrets:* the mar-
tyring Christians scraped the flesh off Hypatia's bones with oyster shells.

earthmother goddess into a chaste mother of a martyred god.

Whose teachings they converted into an orthodox church.

Which converted heresy   a word that used to mean: choice of a view of life other than the norm   into the crime of otherness. Punishable by torture.

—The sudden heresy of astrology.

Which St. Augustine repudiated   together with the suddenly heretic Christianity of the Manichees, & the pagan philosophy of the Greeks   after the repudiated stars warned him of the sudden heresy of all his former beliefs. & sources of knowledge.

As they warned Theron, Alexandria's foremost Greek astrologer & mathematician, of the impending martyrdom of his only daughter. The 45-year-old Greek philosopher Hypatia.

Whose chart Theron had cast at the moment of her birth. Taking pride in her strong Mercury   that promised eloquent intelligence   in fortunate aspect to her Jupiter. That gave her early recognition, a renown greater than his own. Rejoicing at her Moon exalted in the sign of the Bull, which made her clear strong voice turn logic into music. Shaking his head at her Venus in the sign of the Ram, which made her willful in matters of emotion & aesthetics.

Although he had to smile when he recognized that willful Venus in his 4-year-old daughter's request to wear golden sandals on her feet.

& when the 12-year-old started to bind her thick red hair in golden nets.

He was still smiling   though with thinner lips   when the already renowned young philosopher started to have lovers.

Whose charts he also cast.

& when she married the philosopher Isidore. Whose charted philosophical acquiescence to his willful wife's many amorous friendships made Theron shake his head. & wonder if his brilliant daughter was perhaps abusing the power over men seemingly granted to her by the stars.

Which seemed to turn against her, suddenly, as she approached her 45th year. When the lined-up planets foreshadowed an event of such horror that Theron's civilized early-5th-century mind refused to believe what he saw in her progressions.

Which he recast & recast, until belief in his science outweighed his belief in civilized early-5th-century humanity. & he warned his daughter. Urging her to slip out of the city. To travel to Sicily, perhaps, where earlier Greek philosophers had lived out disgraced lives in quiet meditation, & discreet teaching.

But Hypatia refused to listen to her father.

Or perhaps she did listen, but refused to leave a city that used to sit at her feet, listening to her learning. That seemed to be the only city in her civilized world. Where her current lover lived also.

Or perhaps Hypatia was sensing the end of an era, beyond which she had no desire to live.

Her era, that had allowed her to be learned. More learned than her learned astrologer/mathematician father Theron. Than her philosopher husband Isidore.

& to share her learning. With students as illustrious as Synesius of Cyrene. The only Christian she knew to laugh a hearty laugh. Who had just recently become Bishop of Ptolomais. Who was writing her many affectionate, admiring letters.

An era that had allowed a woman to think. & to become known because of her thoughts.

That allowed the known thinking woman to have lovers, besides having a philosophical/philosopher husband.

Powerful lovers, like Orestes, the pagan prefect of Egypt. Her current lover, whom she refused to leave behind in Alexandria.

Whom the Christian gossip of that city had taking orders from his known philosopher-mistress. Whom gossip suspected of being behind the pagan prefect's opposition to Alexandria's Christian patriarch St. Cyril.

Who denied having expressed the un-Christian wish to see the accursed woman dead. To his reader Peter.

Who denied having repeated the Christian patriarch's unexpressed un-Christian wish   casually,   after a mass   to a group of lingering clergy.

Who denied having mentioned the known 45-year-old philosopher by name, in various exhortations

—about the adulterous conduct of pagan wives   the insidious influence of adulterous sex on the minds of pagan politicians, which had led to the martyrdom of earlier Christians in the past—

addressed to various gatherings of their faithful.

Who stopped the unmentioned known 45-year-old philosopher's carriage on its way to her lecture hall. & forced it to go instead to their Christian church of Caesareum.

Where the gathered faithful pulled the philosopher from her carriage.

By the long red hair. In its habitual net of fine gold, that instantly disappeared beneath a faithful cloak.

& by the feet   with their polished toenails   in their habitual golden leather sandals. That instantly disappeared.

& by her tunic. Which tore. & left her nude.

Standing   for another instant   staring wide-eyed across a sea of bodies   that were pausing briefly, getting ready to charge   into the new Christian era in which she'd had no desire to live.

Until she realized how long it took a healthy 45-year-old woman's body to be torn fingers from hands from wrists from elbows from shoulders   toes from feet from ankles from knees from thighs. For the 45-year-old heart to stop beating. For her brain to lose its exceptional consciousness.

OUR LADY
OF THE
EASELS
SUZANNE
VALADON

September 23, 1865*–
April 9, 1938

Go & buy one of my self-portraits if you want to know what I looked like.

I often used myself as a model. It was cheaper than paying someone to sit for me, & more interesting . . . to me. Besides, I had a better-proportioned, more dynamic body than most other girls who posed for the painters on Montmartre.

For whom I used to pose also.

I posed for Henri de Toulouse-Lautrec, who became my closest friend, & the first person to take me seriously, when I showed him some of the drawings I'd been doing.

Which he made me sign Suzanne   instead of Marie-Clémentine   Valadon, as had been my name up to then, given to me by my mother & the parish priest in the porcelain province of the Limousin, where I was born, but never lived. Henri became

---

*As she grew older, Suzanne Valadon refused to be born before 1867, a wish respected by most museums & biographers.

my first customer, & he made me show my drawings to Degas, who said that he recognized me as "one of their own."

That was the beginning. From then on I started thinking of myself as an artist. & a very good one at that. People who didn't like me much, because I was too unpredictable for them, too natural, not refined, like some of my lovers   —like Puvis de Chavannes, for instance—   used to say that I had an ego as big as Sacré Coeur, the church of the wedding cake school of architecture on top of Montmartre, where I lived most of my life. They thought that I was arrogant, saying that I was good. Renoir said I was arrogant when I said that he'd broken off our brief affair because he was jealous of my drawing talent. Which he was. He was always talking religion, but he had a petty streak. & he constantly worried about what people thought or said about him.

Renoir also said that I was not his favorite model   —after I stopped posing for him, after he stopped being my lover—   because I was too short. & that I had a foul mouth that made him forget that I was beautiful.

Which I was: short but beautiful. I had a perfect body, & wide-set dark-grey eyes with stiff dark lashes.   —Until I grew old. But even then I painted myself. I don't know of any other paint-ers   female *or* male   who looked at themselves as objectively as I looked at myself, painting my portrait when I was 63. A self-hatred portrait that was telling the world to go to hell.

Where the world was going anyway then, when I was 63, without my telling it to. My husband André Utter certainly was; he was running, not going. Spending *my* money on booze & other women. Making a fool of himself in every bar, restaurant, & street of Montmartre.

He always came running back to me afterwards, crying to be forgiven. & I always forgave him. I'm not a grudge bearer, like more refined members of this society. I've always believed in kindness & generosity. & André had once been the love of my life.

I left Paul Mousis

—Paul was a banker, who'd set me up in a huge house with a big beautiful garden all around it. & he'd sent my son Maurice to a very fine school. Which eventually expelled my son for being drunk in class.—

to start life anew with André. When I was 43! It's true, I'd been getting bored, living respectably away from Montmartre, & André was exciting. Which was good, because excitement always made me paint.

André was 2 years younger than my son Maurice, whose friend he was when I met him. One of the few friends my poor Maurice ever had. He was extremely well educated; I loved the way he talked. Although later all his big words used to annoy me. They made me feel that he was trying to show up my ignorance.

André was a painter also. But his work never amounted to much. It was too self-conscious, too cerebral. We used to paint together, side by side, during the good years. Which lasted until André insisted that we get married before he had to go off to war in 1914. I hadn't wanted to marry   him or anybody. Why spoil a passionate relationship by pledging to make it last. We'd had fights before   —especially after my son Maurice came to paint alongside us in the studio—   but they'd always ended in passionate reconciliations. We did have one brief span of happiness despite being married when André came home on furlough   — which we spent gloriously, in the country—   but when he came back for good, after the war was over, I was becoming successful, & he couldn't take it.

He was even more outraged by the even greater success   & higher praise, & prices   of the work done by my son Maurice.

—Utrillo, as my son Maurice ended up signing his work. After the death of my Spanish architect lover, who had made a huge fuss over adopting my son Maurice. Which no one had asked him to do. I least of all. It was nobody's business who'd been the father of my son. Besides, it would have made more sense if my son had continued to sign his paintings: Maurice Valadon. He had learned his painting from me, painting next to me, from the beginning.

Which is the best way to learn how to paint, from being around painters. That was how I got started. It's much better than André's formal academic education. André had nothing but contempt for my son's paintings. Those blunt, uniform copies of picture postcards: he used to call them. Which the formal, academy-trained critics were praising, while his own work went ignored.

Their friendship had come to an end long before Maurice became successful, though. I think it stopped when Maurice joined me & André in my studio. There'd be the three of us, lined up behind our easels, painting elbow to elbow. Maurice painting much faster than either of us, almost mechanically: walls & houses, mostly; Sacré Coeur over & over, after a picture postcard.

The Unholy Trinity, the neighbors used to call us, because of all the fighting & screaming they'd hear coming from the studio. Especially when Maurice was entrapped in one of his rages. When he'd tear the place apart, or lean out the window, yelling obscenities if he spotted a pregnant woman somewhere in the street. Sometimes he'd rush out & chase her.

My son was always in & out of police stations. & later in & out of mental institutions. But I don't think we realized how seriously ill he was until the day he deliberately ran head-on into a wall in a police station, in an attempt to kill himself.

He'd had tantrums   alternating with periods of staring into space   even as a child. When my mother used to try calming him with red wine, to stop him from breaking her beloved porcelain figurines. Perhaps she'd also put brandy in his milk bottle to make him stop crying when he was still a baby. Anyway, my son was an alcoholic by the time he turned 12.

Perhaps I shouldn't have given my son to my mother to raise. She was drinking heavily by the time Maurice was born, & she never went anywhere without her brandy bottle. I'd been supporting her   & myself   since before I was 10 years old. Doing all kinds of things.

Montmartre was still an independent community then, separate from Paris, & lots of artists were moving there because it was cheap. They frequented the bars & restaurants, & soon new bars & new restaurants were opening, followed by cabarets, even a circus. The one-time "Hill of the Martyrs," where St. Denis had wandered, carrying his cut-off head in the crook of one arm, was turning from mortification to gratification of the flesh. Most places knew me, & liked me. I was their mascot, their holy little terror. They'd give me leftovers, & let me take food home to my mother as well. Sometimes I'd draw pictures on the pavement, & artists would come by & give me their small change. But that was long before I began to think of myself as a painter.

When I was 16, I convinced the director of the new circus to let me fill in for the trapeze artist who'd gotten sick. I had no training, but he knew I was nimble, & wild, he finally let me do it. Unfortunately I fell off. There was no net. I could have been killed, or maimed for life, but I came out all right. ·It just hurt very much, & attracted a lot of attention.

By the time Maurice was born I was modeling for all the artists who knew me. I was also beginning to take my own drawing more seriously. I couldn't have continued doing that   supporting my mother & me   & taken care of a baby. Besides, my mother was always at home, drinking. She never went anywhere. It seemed natural to let her watch over my son.

To whom she became quite attached, as long as he remained little. She used to call him her Christmas present, because his birthday was on December 26. Whereas *my* attachment started later, when I had to worry about him constantly when his rages got more & more violent. & he remained almost childishly attached to me. Even as a grown man he'd hold on to me, or hold my hand, when we were out together in the street, or in a restaurant.

Until my one-time friend Lucie Valore-Pauwels took him from me, by marrying him, after she was widowed. He was 54 years old by then, & losing him to that snake in the grass made me lose my famous strength.

Which people around me used to find incredible. Enviable. They'd shade their eyes, or put their hands over their ears, when

77

I'd be up & bouncing in the mornings, after a night of drinking with them. When they'd be out flat, & groaning. I was like an island, in a sea of alcoholics. My friend Henri de Toulouse-Lautrec could outdrink anybody on Montmartre, but eventually he out-drank himself & died in 1901, when he was only 37. My mother used to float through the apartment like a blind mass. My son Maurice was either screaming, or staring into space. My husband André Utter turned stupid, literally, as in stupefaction. Whereas I was always full of energy. I was never sick, until I had to go to the hospital with uremic poisoning, when I was 68. When my "friend" Lucie promised to take care of my son if anything should happen to me. But I got well & she proceeded to steal my son. After that, my body went steadily downhill. I felt abandoned, & lonely, even after that dear boy Gazi came to Paris to take care of me.

Gazi had been a teenager the year I & André had vacationed in the country during the war, during André's furlough. When I had been the great mysterious lady painter from Paris to the boy. Perhaps he came to bury an adolescent fantasy of his when he moved in with me. & he did bury me. He was holding my hand in the ambulance that was driving me to my death.

Come to think of it, there probably isn't a painting of mine for sale anywhere, let alone a self-portrait. & if you did find one, you probably couldn't afford to buy it. I've become very expensive. The greatest woman painter in France: that's what it says about me in the catalogues & encyclopedias. I always thought so myself; now everyone agrees. You may have to settle for reproductions in art books   or for a photograph of me in my twenties, wearing the new hat my friend Henri de Toulouse-Lautrec had just bought me   if you still want to know what I looked like.

VIRTUOSA
DOMESTICA
CLARA
SCHUMANN,
NÉE WIECK

September 13, 1819–
May 29, 1896

Before the birth of his first child father Wieck decides that he will have a musician, even if the child is a girl. She is, & he names her Clara. As in: limpid   pure sound perfect pitch. As in Clarinet.

At the age of 5 she takes her seat beside him in front of the piano. By the time she's 9, she's ready to give her first concert, at 11 her first complete recital.

She is becoming the accomplished musician her father envisioned. & molded. & manages. She's not only a virtuosa pianist, she also sings   plays the violin   reads scores   &   — this is most important to him—   composes her own songs & piano pieces.

All of Europe knows her name: Clara Wieck. The great of her time applaud & admire her: Goethe   Mendelssohn   Chopin   Liszt   Grillparzer   Paganini.   & Robert Schumann. Who follows up on his applause & admiration: He moves in with Clara's family. To the distress of the molding father, who hates to see his growing vision eventually go to waste as the wife of another musician.

For seven years Robert Schumann waits for Clara to turn 18, to become old enough to be asked in marriage. By this time the father's distress has swollen to a loathing of irrational proportions. He accuses Robert Schumann of perversions only a parent is able to detect in the lover-robber of his wonderchild. Of a daughter who may feel that she will not be able to fulfill her father's expectations. Which may feel stifling to her, hostile to her fulfillment as a woman.

Whose 18-year-old "we" no longer refers to the musical duo of herself & her father   —who taught her all she knows; who set up her concerts & watched over her performances from the wings; who devoted his life to hers—   but to a perversely patient other musician. Whose admiring courtship the fault-detecting father foresees as becoming censorship, once the marriage is concluded. He foresees the composer-husband convincing his talented wife that writing music is a creative talent reserved for men.

"I once thought that I possessed creative talent, but I have given up this idea: a woman must not desire to compose   — Not one has been able to do it, and why should I expect to? It would be arrogance, although, indeed, my father led me into it in earlier days," the bride-to-be writes in her diary.

At that time she had just become a party in a 3-year legal battle. Robert Schumann & the dissenting daughter are suing her father for slander. & for the permission to marry. After 3 years the courts give them the blessing her father will not give. Clara Wieck is 21 when she becomes Clara Schumann for the rest of her life.

& becomes instantly dismayed:

By the absolute silence her husband requires throughout their house while he composes.   —Which excludes doing any work of her own.

By his increasing nervousness, alternating with extramarital absences.

By the clockwork of conjugal sex: 3 times a week.   —Which produces 8 children in 14 years.

By the obstacles children are to performing & composing.   —She composes less & less, but she performs constantly, despite her children. Sometimes so close to an impending delivery that audiences expect to see a baby musician materialize under her piano stool.

Perhaps it is a relief for Clara Schumann when her nervous, maniacally irritable husband is committed to a mental institution. At least it frees her from continuous childbearing.

Besides, another musician has recently come into her life: Johannes Brahms. He is 14 years younger than she is. & writes her that he loves her better than himself. He will   & does   remain her close friend for life.

She plays & promotes his compositions alongside her husband's compositions all over Europe. She is performing more than ever, to pay the hospital bills for her steadily deteriorating husband.

—Who never mentions Clara   not even the fact that he has a wife   to the doctor who treats him.   (also for tertiary syphilis)   & strictly forbids Clara to visit her husband during the 2 years he continues his treatment, but then urgently summons her hours before his death.

For which she is branded a heartless wife, by frowning contemporaries. Who dislike a strong-willed woman, a wife who receives intimate letters from another   younger   musician, while her poor unvisited husband lies lingering in a madhouse.

Where he was probably driven by his heartless   probably adulterous   wife.

Whom the frowning contemporaries see also as an impossible mother. Who thinks of herself as a performer & a public figure first & foremost, as a wife second, a daughter third, & only fourth as a mother.

Stravinsky   who met Clara Schumann when he was 13 & she quite an old woman, still gregarious despite rheumatism & hearing problems   placed her first on his list of disastrous wives.

A
GREAT-WALL
FLOWER
MU-LAN
HWA

My father was a court physician who doubled as a general in the Imperial Army in times of war. In times of peace he took care of the old Emperor's health.

In those days a doctor was paid as long as his patients stayed healthy, but not when they fell ill. For which they blamed their doctor.

Although no one blamed my father when the old Emperor died, of old age, he left the court & withdrew to the provinces, where he visited sick farmers in their often distant houses.

On one such visit he was led to the bed of a white-faced young woman who was ill with pneumonia. He treated her, & when she recovered they married.

I arrived in due course.

As soon as I was born my mother sent for the wise man to consult the cowrie shells about my life.

I wish I'd been old enough to see the dignified seer do a crane dance on his spindly old legs. Before throwing himself at my baby feet, drooling abject veneration. Muttering: Great feats . . . great honors . . . an extraordinary life.

The most extraordinary was that he refused to accept any form of payment for his consultation.

I grew up thinking that I had seen it all, with my one-day-old eyes, I was told about it so many times:

By my mother, until she died giving birth to a dead little boy, when I was 5. I remember her bending down to me, repeating: an extraordinary life . . . an extraordinary life . . . Her face always was a translucent white, even without powder.

By my nurse who would have liked to place me on a pedestal, like an Imperial vase, to preserve me for my impending honors.

Even by my father, who was raising me to be "a valiant scholar." A   poet/painter/calligrapher/musician/soldier/military strategist. I rode a fast horse by the time I was 11, & started winning at swordplay when I turned 13. Perhaps my father was getting old, or perhaps he let me win to boost my confidence in the fate that was awaiting me.

That kept me waiting. For 17 years I woke up every morning expecting the extraordinary to begin, & every evening I went to bed disappointed.

When it did begin, finally, I was asleep. It was early morning. My nurse roused me with whispers of panic. What were we to do! An Imperial messenger was calling on my father to resume his duties as general. Barbarian invaders needed to be driven out. But my father was not there. My father was visiting patients. What were we to do? What were we to do?!!

I told her to feed the Imperial messenger. While he ate I would put on my father's battledress, & assume my father's role.

She looked horrified, but she didn't protest. The wise man's prediction was ringing in her ears.

I presented myself to the Imperial messenger, who didn't seem surprised by the youth of his general. If he was he didn't show it. He was to be my adjutant, he said, & we rode off side by side.

When I found out that he was the Emperor's youngest son, I secretly pledged to shield him from injury. With my life, if necessary. I felt patriotic, but I was fooling myself. He could have been anybody's son, a bastard, & I'd have wanted to protect him. I had fallen in love.

I felt that he loved me also, although he didn't know it, or it would have troubled him. Perhaps he did know it, & he hid his trouble from me as deceitfully as I hid being a woman. Which required a lot of deviousness at times.

For 5 years we fought the Barbarian invaders, until I finally lured them back behind their border. A strategy of circumvention & wedge attack from the rear that sacrificed relatively few lives, & earned me high praise.

The Emperor received us most graciously. I was his most ingenious young general: he said. & offered me one of his 3 daughters in marriage, as a reward.

They were present, & inspected me from head to toe, deciding who would like me best. The Imperial messenger embraced me like a brother. I burst into tears, wishing for a butterfly sleeve.

The Imperial messenger rushed to my rescue. Battle fatigue, he said, he, too, was suffering from it. & would weep, if he had the courage.

The Emperor requested to be left alone with me. The court withdrew. I threw myself at his feet. I was not who he thought I was: I stammered.

Who did I think he thought I was?

My father.

No. I looked too young to be my father. Whom he had known a quarter of a century ago. A man too old to go to war. He knew that I had taken my father's place.

Yes, but . . .

That was noble of me. I was an example of filial devotion, well worthy of marrying an imperial daughter.

But I couldn't possibly . . .

& why not? Did not one of his daughters look pleasing to me? What an insult to their father.

His tone was harsh, but I sensed a smile behind his words. Perhaps he knew that I was a woman, since he knew my father.

Perhaps he had known it all along, & was playing with me. It made me furious. I rose to my feet. I was a woman: I said hotly: My name was Mu-Lan. Mu-Lan Hwa. I couldn't possibly marry another woman.

So that was it. Well, in that case, how would I like to marry one of his sons.

He was laughing now, & I started laughing with him, relieved to be myself again.

A week later I married his youngest son, the Imperial messenger, my beloved comrade in arms. My father returned from the provinces & took up residence at court again as one of the Emperor's physicians. & I, at least, have lived happily ever after.

Allegedly my heroic life took place somewhere between the beginning of the North Wei dynasty (A.D. 386) & the end of the Sui dynasty (A.D. 618).

But perhaps I'm a myth. The legendary woman warrior who has lived in the heart of every Chinese girl born between my death & 1911. Whose toes were broken, & rebroken, & bound under her soles to prevent healing, after an arthritic Tang empress decreed that women had to hobble like her if they wanted to be received at court.

For more than 1,000 years women's absurd painful baby steps remained a symbol of affluence for their fathers & husbands.

I, Mu-Lan Hwa, am those women's collective dream. A dream of walking, & running, & standing on tiptoe that finally came true.

HAVE YOU
ASKED THE
LEPER IF HE
WANTS
YOUR KISS?
SIMONE
WEIL

February 3, 1909– The exceptional, like the average,
August 22, 1943 have usually average parents/
classmates. Friends. Who often
feel more average, compared to their exceptional child/classmate.
Friend.

May you never have a child who is a saint: Simone Weil's
mother tells a biographer, recalling the apprentice-saint's childhood pranks:

Little Simone, persuading her brother who is 9 months
older than she is, with whom she shares a private world to go
to neighbors' houses during a vacation in the country, begging
for food.

Telling the astonished neighbors that their parents, the good
doctor Weil & his kind wife, are not so good or kind at home.
That they are starving their children. Which looks believable to
the astonished neighbors: Both children look convincingly
scrawny.

They eat what the neighbors feed them, & run home laughing,
to tell their parents.

Or: Little Simone, refusing to wear socks in winter, persuading her brother-accomplice to do the same. Blue-legged they sit in the subway between their parents. Don't you wish our parents would buy us nice warm socks, Simone says for the whole subway car to hear. Her brother nods sadly, & sighs. Accusing subway riders' eyes fasten on the parents' faces.

These are the amusements of a child who refuses to accept a ring, when she is 3 years old, explaining that: She doesn't like luxuries.

Who asks the family doctor, when she is 5 & gravely ill, not to give her sedatives. She wants to be fully awake, in case she should die. She is determined not to waste her death: she says to the awed doctor. Who despairs of saving her. A 5-year-old, saying such things . . .

She recovers, but her relationship to her body remains strained. It is a body she neither enjoys nor respects. That houses her exceptional mind at the price of headaches, which become so violent, she has fantasies of bashing people on the forehead. Of stomach cramps that make eating distasteful. Of hands that are too small, & swollen from bad circulation. They hurt when she writes.

Yet she writes continuously.

Like a typewriter: according to the philosopher Alain, her teacher at the *école normale*. Who calls her: The Martian, because of her blunt dress & manner. But his respect for her increases with each paper she writes for his course.

Perhaps it is his influence that makes her choose philosophy as her career. But gradually her admiration for his teachings decreases. She considers his "rejection of pain" a shortcoming, as she continues to ignore her body.

A badly cut-off piece of God is what she calls herself. With the same bluntness with which she tells everyone everything she thinks under all circumstances.

Embarrassing everyone:

The maid she insists on overpaying. Perhaps in defiance of her protective parents who try to impose a few basic comforts on her life, to preserve her body against her will.

The conservative school principals in the provincial town where she is given her first job, teaching philosophy. Where she blatantly marches with the striking workers. To whom she also gives free classes in mathematics.

The local newspapers call her: The Red Virgin.

The Spanish freedom fighters whom she insists on joining. Into whose boiling stew she nearsightedly walks, inflicting a slow-healing injury on her leg. Spoiling their meal.

The workers at the Renault Factory, where she insists on taking her place with those at the bottom. Where the affliction of others enters her flesh & soul, as she receives forever the mark of slavery . . . It seems to those who obey that some mysterious inferiority predestines them to obey for all eternity . . . What lowers the intelligence degrades the entire person . . .

Where she earns   & lives on   next to nothing, not allowing her parents to help her, because a true rebel is morally & materially alone.

She is paid by the piece, & much slower than the regular workers. Who do not necessarily appreciate a young philosophy professor working ineptly among them. Holding them up with her clumsiness & political idealism.

Which is shattered by the workers' lack of solidarity. Although she understands them: It is difficult to judge from above, & it is difficult to act from below . . .

She begins to think that politics are a sinister farce.

The farmers, whose roughest work she insists on sharing, while refusing to share their food . . . As long as people in the cities must live on ration cards . . .

Who hadn't realized they were so pitiful, until she came to help them.

Whose tractor she insists on driving, & promptly overturns. Infuriating the driver, whom she vainly tries to appease with offerings of cigarettes.

Which are also rationed. But which she somehow manages to obtain in sufficient quantities.

Cigarettes are Simone Weil's only luxury. The only indulgence she allows herself, as she lives more & more in the poverty of those who are searching.

Her political idealism has turned into religious quest. She feels deeply drawn to Catholicism, yet she hesitates to let herself be baptized. The Church as social structure frightens her. She wants no part of Church patriotism. Of the twofold Roman-Hebraic tradition that has negated the divine inspiration of Christianity for 2,000 years . . .

To Simone Weil the era of enlightenment took place during the 11th & 12th centuries, & ended with the extermination of the Cathari, a religious sect that blended the teachings of Christ, Buddha, & Zoroaster into a single message of peace. Which automatically invited their persecution by religious & secular powers alike. Their compassion for all living beings appeals to Simone Weil, as does their belief that it was a sin to create new life, to force a spirit to become flesh. . . . Leaves & fruits are a waste of energy for a tree that wants to grow only higher . . .

The Cathari sometimes tolerated a practice known as *la endura,* death by starvation, although they did not encourage it. Perhaps Simone Weil's controversial death   —by starvation, according to the autopsy—   was such an *endura.* An act of withdrawal from the flesh does not seem out of character for a badly cut-off piece of God.

Who wrote *Gravity and Grace.*

Who wrote: "The man who does not wear the armor of the lie cannot experience violence without being touched by it to his very soul. Grace can spare the touch from corrupting him, but it cannot spare him the wound . . .

"To die [for something] does not commit one to anything. If one can say such a thing. It does not contain anything in the nature of a lie . . ."

Grace rises from Simone Weil's writings like a subtle perfume, the *odeur de sainteté* hagiographers unmistakably detect when they describe the mistreated flesh or the undecaying corpses of their saintly subjects.

According to numerology, Simone Weil's path of life is 6/33.

February 3, 1909

$$2 + 3 + 19 + 9 = 33$$

6 stands for: the womb   the house   sudden marriage or divorce. It also stands for *initiation by ordeal*. A painfully initiated 6 may function on its higher octave 33, the exceptional master number of sainthood.

A
VICTORIAN
PINUP
(SPEAKS OUT)
FANNY
KEMBLE

November 27, 1809–
January 15, 1893

Which talents flourish best? Talents that grow in obscurity, like flower bulbs in a cellar. That need outside intervention to bring them to light. Talents sown into hostile environments that spend years of energy tunneling through family prisons before they burst into expression like trees of heaven exploding from city cement.

Or those who, like Fanny Kemble, seem to have chosen their parents in preparation for early stardom. Which they seem to claim with their first smile   their first word   their first step.

Talents that grow into crowns on top of their parents' professions, which they seem to learn by osmosis, even when they're educated in boarding schools in France, & the parents work in the theatre in London.

Fanny Kemble's father was not only a prominent British actor, he also managed Covent Garden Theatre, where his 20-year-old daughter played Juliet, & was propelled to instant fame by her first performance. For three years all of theatre-going Victorian

England lay at the young actress's feet, & she decided to tour America, to extend her circle of admirers.

Young stars who chose their parents career-wisely, preparatorily, often choose mates who seem to counteract their initial sense of direction. Men who like the notion of being married to a star, but then expect their wife to sparkle for them alone; at most for an audience of selected dinner guests.

Fanny Kemble gave up acting to marry Pierce Butler, a rich Philadelphian, who owned large plantations in Georgia, & hundreds of slaves. He may have appeared to her like a mythical prince, ruling over vast areas of lush unknown vegetation, in the new world she had come to visit.

Their first meeting may have been an exchange of audiences: The visiting star receiving homage from a resident prince; the resident prince opening his palace to a visiting star.

She may not have associated the homage-paying prince with the strangely primitive customs & peculiar institutions that disconcerted her in the new world. Even though she knew that much of his wealth was derived from the new world's most peculiar institution: slavery.

Or perhaps she'd felt confident that his princely intelligence could not fail to realize the superiority of her own old-world ways & values.

While he may have felt confident that her star-brightness could not fail to agree that a wife was a wife, in his new or any other conceivable world.

For the next 10 years their marriage became a battlefield for increasingly diverging ideologies & personal cross purposes. Pierce Butler soon grew tired of coaxing his ex-star to act the wifely foil to which he felt entitled. While the ex-star   —who had felt at least equal to her prince during their mutual granting of audiences—   felt entitled to continued equality as his wife.

& to her opinions. Which she felt entitled to express publicly, since he refused to listen. In a book published 1 year after their marriage: *Journal of a Residence in America.* It became a best-selling embarrassment to her husband, & disconcerted many contemporary readers with its "racy" language.

Eventually, the desolation of her exiled life, parallel to an increasingly disgusted husband, whose life she touched only in battle, became unbearable. & pointless. She left him   & their 2 daughters   & resumed her acting career in London.

She was still a star, although less adulated, at 35, than she had been after her debut at 20.

4 years later Pierce Butler filed for divorce, & she rushed back to America.

Perhaps using the divorce threat as a pretext to return. A strange thing happens to Europeans who come to live in America.   — Perhaps to immigrants from & to anywhere.—   They find it difficult to readapt to life in their own countries. Even if their American life was one long unfavorable comparison to "home." Which no longer felt like home, after their return. & they prefer to rush back to where they don't feel as strange when they feel like strangers.

Even though Fanny Kemble died in London   —at the age of 83—   during one of her frequent visits there, most of her life after 40 was spent in America.

At first she continued to work as an actress   —though under less starlike conditions—   giving public readings of Shakespeare. But then she switched to writing: memoirs, literary criticism, poetry, drama, & finally a novel which was published when she was 80.

The most successful of her books was another best-selling embarrassment to Pierce Butler: *Journal of a Residence on a Georgian Plantation,* published in 1863. It is a passionate denunciation of slavery, which she found especially painful for the slave women, "whose sorrow-laden existence and continual childbearing appeared to be all in a day's work." She depicted their life with a brutal realism that again disconcerted many contemporary readers.

Although Fanny Kemble is given credit mainly as a Victorian pinup of the London Stage, she deserves at least equal billing as a chronicler of 19th-century America. As an outspoken critic of the institutions of slavery, & of marriage.

REMNANTS

OF AN

UNKNOWN

WOMAN

STELLINA

July 6, 1907–
February ?, 1970

We call it litter when we see it being dropped. & we pass laws against the droppers. But when we stumble upon it, years   centuries   millennia   later,   we carefully gather it up   collect it   sift it   label it   catalogue it, & base on it the scientific invention of the passage of man which we call: History.

The streets of New York City are littered with seeds of history. Weeds of history. Thrown-out shards of anonymous lives which remain as mysterious to the finder   & as pertinent to the human condition & its era   as a Mayan inscription.

—Which, for all we know, may have been a copy of The Mayan Daily News.

Papers   postcards   photographs   spill from a garbage can on 8th Street & Avenue B on a drizzly February evening. Unclaimed leftovers of a life, thrown out by a super, perhaps, who had orders to rent the apartment   perhaps only the room vacated by the death of a woman who had lived alone.

Her name is Stellina
—daughter of Celestina, a Small Star fallen from   dropped
by   a Small Sky, or Small Heaven.—

Large Italian features on a short sturdy neck. Her mouth is a
tight line, as serious as the British passport for which she is being
photographed. To travel to America, at the age of 40. The thick
dark eyebrows repeat the seriousness of the mouth. It *is* serious,
leaving what she has known for 40 years to go to a huge city where
she knows no one.

Why was Stellina born in Liverpool, England, when her photographed family looks solidly grounded in Sicily. In a much-
photographed stone house surrounded by orchards. Against a blue
backdrop of sky.

—Where she sends money: to add to the surrounding orchards.—

Why did the 40-year-old Stellina decide to emigrate from England to America?

—After Mr. Sciascia's restaurant closed in Liverpool, England.
Where she had worked as a cook for 25 years, ever since she
turned 15: according to a letter of reference.—

Why had she not gone to live with her photographed mother,
the Little Sky/the Little Heaven in the orchard-surrounded stone
house in the Sicilian sunshine. Where all the photographed others
live: 2 photographed younger sisters with their 2 photographed
husbands, & 1 photographed younger brother with his 1 photographed wife, & glossy nieces & nephews on baptism/first-
communion studio photographs.

—Which cost money, Stellina. Children are expensive, Stellina. You're lucky, having only yourself to take care of, in money-
country America. Where everything's electric, down to the
chairs.—

Where Stellina becomes a fruit packer.

Was Stellina born in Liverpool, England, because Mr. Sciascia   —or a close friend of Mr. Sciascia, or a close relation—
had been implicated in her birth. & became a benefactor

when he became her boss in his Italian restaurant in Liverpool.

Had Celestina, the Little Sky/the Little Heaven spent time in Liverpool, England. & returned to Sicily to get married & raise a legitimate family after dropping an illegitimate Little Star. Who had to be left behind, if the Little Sky/the Little Heaven was to make a legitimate new life for herself.

& had the 40-year-old Little Star come to America to escape her British illegitimacy. Which had perhaps felt like a sin to her. Not her heavenly mother Celestina's sin, but her own.

2 framed photographs of the mother show a more graceful, less stone-faced woman than those   unframed   of the daughter.

On the passport, Stellina's grey-streaked hair is knotted into a grim British bun.

Which she cuts   dyes   perms   as she adapts to America. & learns to smile when she is photographed. In the company of 4 other 40-year-old "girls," less sturdy-necked, less thick-ankled fruit packers, on a Sunday pilgrimage to Lourdes in the Bronx.

Stellina, a reconstructed solitude. A thrown-out application form reveals her   perhaps unfulfilled   ambition: to be promoted from fruit packer to tomato packer.

A SENSITIVE GIANT

LADY

OTTOLINE

(VIOLET ANNE CAVENDISH-BENTICK; MARRIED TO PHILIP)

MORELL

June 16, 1883–
April 21, 1938

Much of my life was spent feeling out of place, in my time as much as in my country, although the roots of my family have royal extensions and intertwine with the history of England.

I remember feeling proud of not being proud of my historical name, as a young and friendless, very lonely girl. When I used to be painfully shy, and deeply religious, holding prayer meetings with the servants.

I remained religious throughout my life. It was a source of many unhappy arguments, many of them with Bertie Russell, who fully shared and encouraged my active opposition to war (in 1914), but had little use for the teachings of the Lord of Peace. (His sharp objections were made sharper still by his terrible breath. I never told him, not even at a distance in any of the 1,500 letters I wrote him in response to his 2,000, that his breath made kissing him an ordeal.)

And I continued to be plagued by fits of shyness, especially in the presence of those clever, immensely capable women who always seemed to know exactly what to do, and to say, and to wear. They always seemed to be sitting in judgment of me, making me feel that I looked peculiar, dressed as a nymph or a shepherdess, too colorful in my dull-violet dress with the green sleeves   (I wore it to meet Joseph Conrad, who approved of it)   or my embroidered canary-yellow silk coat, or my large, feathered hats.

The 10-year-old son of one of these women, then my houseguest in the country, actually asked me one morning (the child obviously echoing the parent): "Why are you wearing so many things?" Making me feel even less clever and capable, unsuited to work for the good causes I wished to help, needlessly reminding me of my inadequacy, of the thought that my life might be useless which never ceased to haunt me, despite my constant attempts to make an art of life. I was a battlefield for an endless civil war between puritanism and beauty.

I desperately needed beauty around me, and went looking for it everywhere, in nature, in my clothes, my houses, my pugs and peacocks; the sepia ink in which I wrote all my letters, my diaries, and eventually my memoirs.

And of course I was looking for beauty in the many artists, thinkers, and writers whom I invited to my open house on Thursdays and to the country during the summers, whom I encouraged and actively helped, often supporting them for extended periods.

I think my admiration for D. H. Lawrence, based on his earlier writings, turned to love during a walk we took together, when I found in him the same vividness with which I felt the wind, and the flowers.

He was also extremely sensitive to my aristocratic background, although that did not stop him later from making a caricature of me as Hermione in his *Women in Love*. His attitude had changed by then, not only toward me, but also in his writing. I thought he was becoming sloppy and felt ashamed when, reading *The Rainbow*, I counted twelve repetitions of the word fecund on the same page. He was, however, not one to accept criticism, only praise, whereas I always welcomed suggestions, from anyone, after I began writing my memoirs.

Lawrence certainly was not the only one   —although perhaps one of the most hurtful—   to repay my generous interest and hospitality with unkindness. Accusing me of "imposing my will on everyone," including my daughter Julian, who often needed to be sent away because of her delicate health.

It is true that I did not feel suited for motherhood, but when I heard my child's first cry there was an answering cry in me. When the healthier of my twins, our dear little boy, died a few days after his birth, my grief made me all the more fearful for his frailer sister.

It is also true that I often wished to change those in whom I took an active interest, wishing to emphasize their positive, creative sides and alleviate their negative, often self-destructive moods, though even while trying to help I often felt that it probably was a mistake, that the days of patronage were probably over, perhaps even insulting to writers and artists in the 20th century.

Perhaps I belonged to the time of hoops and loops and billowing skirts, although the women who wore them were shorter in those days   —people were shorter then—   whereas I was exceedingly tall for a woman, even in the taller 19th and 20th centuries.

—"So tall . . . so beautiful . . . like a giraffe . . . !" Nijinsky exclaimed when we first met. Everyone laughed, but he liked giraffes, and did think them beautiful. He was paying me a compliment.—

I also had an equine jaw   —that was later badly scarred by a life-saving operation—   and an unwomanly long nose. Not unlike Dante's on the popular busts that are displayed for sale to tourists all over Italy. But a nose that may have flattered the face of a great Italian poet in the 13th and 14th centuries   —with implications of virile prowess—   did not predestine me to be a femme fatale, despite my long very thick golden red hair (the kind of hair that had inspired Botticelli in 15th- and 16th-century Italy). Instead of glamour it only gave me the constant obsession of looking disheveled. (And plain.)

Still, I felt at home in Italy from the instant I set foot on its soil. It became the land of my freedom, the land of my first great love, for the Swedish witch doctor Axel Munthe. I visited him on Capri, scandalizing my female travel companion, and my brothers' family council back home.

It ended in heartbreak   —partly due to my religious convictions—   setting the pattern for most of my future involvements. With the blessed exception of my dear, unfalteringly sympathetic and supportive husband Philip, who loved me so much that he wanted to die first, to hear me say: "I'm coming."

Philip consoled me the many times I was betrayed, by lovers as well as by friends.

By Roger Fry who accused me of spreading the rumor that he was in love with me, during our first reunion, which I had so eagerly anticipated, after his return from Europe. Roger was extremely rude to me then, and he remained rude for a long time afterwards.

By Bertie Russell, who told me that I was getting grey when his passion for me was waning, and he had begun to cast about for other, fertile women to bear his child "before it was too late" (for him). He also said that I was "too much like Blake, and not enough like Shakespeare."

By Virginia Stephen (Woolf), up to then a familiar visitor to my house, who went around saying that I "had the head of a Medusa."

By Lytton Strachey to whom I had given my unreserved friendship and support when he'd been ostracized for his homosexuality, and often suicidal, before he became acclaimed and lionized, when he began telling people that I had no taste, and that the hems of my white angel gowns were caked with mud, and their winglike sleeves stiff with the wiped-off drool from the peppermints to which he claimed I was addicted.

My dearest Philip stood by me throughout, after it became fashionable to ridicule "the Ott," as D. H. Lawrence had taken to calling me then. Philip lovingly subjected himself with me to the infinite boredom that always accompanies the search for health, when we traveled far and wide to visit foreign specialists, when my migraines and stomach cramps increased in frequency and in vigor, and I had to take more and more drugs, which slurred my speech and made completing sentences difficult.

It became another source of mirth for many of my one-time friends and lovers, who may all have to die before posterity may perhaps speak of me as a center of the artistic universe of my time and my country, a generous and passionate supporter, friend, lover, wife, and mother; and a courageous defender of the cause of peace at a time when people gave a white feather to conscientious objectors as a symbol of cowardice.

ANTHONY'S MOM

FRANCES MILTON TROLLOPE

about 1780–
October 6, 1863

Some talents have easy beginnings. They are the treasures of amazed parents who worship the miracle they have produced. They have dedicated teachers. They inspire romance. They know early what they want to do, & when they do it the world applauds.

& perhaps ceases to applaud. Abruptly. Because of a change in perspective. A fashion of reality. & the talents die of injured surprise. Or linger, stretching their dying with memories, like cut flowers kept in water.

Others grow up unnoticed. They take time to discover who they are. & what they want to do. Unsupported. Often supporting untalented others.

& abruptly a change in perspective turns years of obscurity to dazzling light. They grow brighter as they grow older, & die with smiles on their faces.

& each group claims that the other has it easier.

Being born a homely vicar's daughter in Heckfield, 18th-century England, is not an easy beginning. You look like your father. Who looks like Heckfield, from practice of preaching there.

You also inherited his wit. Which still compensates for a lack of looks, in gabby old England. Even in the case of a young woman.

But it does not compensate for marriage. At least not at age 30, when even an unhappy marriage looks better than none.

When it's preferable for Frances Milton to become Mrs. Trollope. & start living beside a surly, abrasive barrister, who becomes surlier as he becomes sickly, & more abrasive with every failed business venture.

You bear 6 sickly children.　　—4 of whom die of consumption at varying ages.—　　& you suffer from migraines, which you try to cure with a laxative: calomel.

One day, the sickly abrasive failure of a man beside whom you've been living for 20 years discovers America. He keeps reading about mediocrities and embezzlers and disreputable sons of reputable families who are making good in the colonies. He doesn't ask, but you agree to travel ahead while he extricates himself from another avalanche of obligations. You will reconnoiter the promised land. In the company of 2 daughters, 1 sickly son, & your good friend, the artist Auguste Hervieu.

You crisscross the country in great discomfort. Meeting many rude Americans, who see only a dowdy old woman　—you're close to 50—　to whom nobody speaks or listens, in the new world. Regardless of her wit. Her knowledge of contemporary literature. Her love of the poets of the past. They're not impressed that you read Dante in the original.

But you're impressed with them. With their rudeness. Their spitting. Their poor table manners. Their bad taste in clothes. Their roaches.

—Which you blame on the Republican form of their government. Under which "Church and State hobble along side by side, notwithstanding their boasted independence."

Finally, Mr. T. & a second sickly son join you in Cincinnati, where you set up a preposterous bazaar, that becomes known as

Trollope's Folly. & fails miserably. You're called: The dowdy and bankrupt Mrs. Trollope, & you recross the Atlantic.

& turn your failed adventure into a *succès de scandale* with the publication of "The Domestic Manners of the Americans." It's your revenge on the rough, uncouth, & vulgar Republicans who looked away when you tried to talk to them.

But who now read what you have to say about them. & hate you for every word. Making you money with their rage. Your publisher prints 4 editions in 1 year.

& you're translated into French & Spanish.

Your British contemporaries also resent your success, though for different reasons: Writing social satire is a man's prerogative. They make you pay for the transgression of your wit.

Shelton publishes a mean booklet about you: Trollopiana, with meaner caricatures by Johnston. Which show you gross-faced, one hand raising your dowdy skirt in a dance step, the other swinging a whiskey bottle, the alleged source of your inspiration & high spirits.

She looks like her name: they say in conclusion.

Mrs. Trollope. The married name with which you signed your best-selling American travelogue.

But their ridicule of you grieves you less than the persecution of Byron. For whom you weep.

You continue to write other books, travelogues interspersed with novels   —between 4 A.M. & the time your household gets up—   which you continue to sign: Mrs. Trollope. During the next 26 years you produce 114 volumes.

Which earn you a great deal of money. With which you support your dying husband. & your sickly & dying children. For whom you buy & furnish 3 different houses in as many years.

& you travel extensively all over Europe. & finally move to Italy, when you're 64, & live in Florence for the rest of your long life.

One of the chapters in your son Anthony's famous posthumous autobiography is about you. He says that: You were extravagant. & most capable of joy.

A LIFE
OF LOVE &
LAUGHTER
MARIE
LAURENCIN

October 1885–
June 8, 1956

An early self-portrait shows Marie Laurencin as a pale, arch-browed young lady with an unusually oval face, mocking lips, a short pointed nose, & black hair hanging heavily against a slender neck. She looks romantic, as Creole even partly Creole women were expected to look in 19th- & early-20th-century Paris.

She also looks amused —perhaps in acknowledgment of being expected to look romantic.

There was nothing romantic or amused about Marie Laurencin's Creole mother. At least not to her small & growing daughter. Whose drawings the mother burned, regularly, throughout her daughter's childhood, way into her lycée years.

An elegant, unromantically formidable mother, whom the adult daughter never dared to ask who her father had been.

But also a conciliatory mother, who allowed her daughter to study drawing at the Académie Hubert, once she had completed her formal lycée education.

& a practical mother, who enrolled the young art student also at the Ecole de Sèvres, to be able to support herself as a porcelain painter.

Which Marie Laurencin might have become, if Georges Braque had not rescued her from mere craftsmanship. He felt that her talent deserved a broader scope, & brought her into the circle that surrounded Picasso.

From that moment on she became the embodiment of the artistic moods of the avant-garde. Although she was an instinctive, "decorative" painter, whose diaphanous young girls & "boneless" animals had very little in common with the increasingly complex abstractions & intellectualizations of the Cubists & later of the Dadaists.

In 1907 Picasso introduced her to Guillaume Apollinaire, saying that he had found him a "fiancée." Perhaps he had. The 27-year-old Apollinaire, an established literary figure, & skirt chaser, & the 22-year-old romantic embodiment of the artistic avant-garde he hung out with, became inseparable for almost 6 years.

Apollinaire claimed that she was his female counterpart: "Easygoing, good-hearted, and witty; a little sun." At whose feet he claimed to be living.

Perhaps they did have many similarities: They were both illegitimate, raised by determined mothers. & they both had endless lovers. But he was jealously possessive   —at least of her— while she believed that love was meant to be a   preferably joyous   meeting of colorful butterflies & pale deep-throated flowers.

Eventually his blatant philandering, alternating with tantrums of jealousy, got the best of her sunny disposition, & she threw him out.

Incurring the wrath of the art critics & art historians of the Cubist-Dadaist movement, who excuse themselves to this day for mentioning her paintings. Which   they say   they mention only because she once was the mistress of Apollinaire. Although they admit that she was the embodiment of her artistic era, no less significantly than the dress designer Chanel.

Gertrude Stein, her very first buyer at her very first show in 1907   —where she had bought the "group portrait of Apollinaire with friends"—   blatantly discontinued her patronage shortly after the much-criticized breakup with Apollinaire.

Six weeks before the outbreak of WWI Marie Laurencin married a former fellow student from the Académie Hubert. A man who happened to be German   & a baron   & a fellow painter who felt that he was the greater, unjustly unrecognized talent in their politically untimely marriage. Which raised many questions from many unsolicited quarters. & inspired Jean Giraudoux to write: *Siegfried et le limousin.*

& forced the couple to flee to Spain. Where they waited out the war. When it was over, Marie Laurencin traveled to Germany & filed for divorce.

But she remained friends with her ex-husband. Whom the war had turned into an impoverished aristocratic alcoholic.

Whereas she resumed her career as a fashionable & prolific painter as soon as she returned to Paris in 1920. & she continued to have men living at her feet, begging her to marry them.

Which she no longer wished to do, after living for almost six years with a jealous philanderer, & for another six years with a competitive drunk. Preferring instead to live with "families of cats." Which led to a legal battle over the ownership of her apartment. She won the lawsuit in the hospital, a few days before she died.

"She was not a great artist, far from it, but a pleasing one," Somerset Maugham said about her after her death. Patronizingly. Perhaps to erase the long nose & fastidious mouth from the portrait she painted of him in 1936.

Which might have flattered him even less if she had painted it in 1937, when she acquired the "establishment glasses," which hardened the nearsighted haze of her world.

Perhaps she should not have given him the portrait. (As she was wont to do, indiscriminately, to her hairdresser, to restaurants, to anyone who didn't feel entitled.) Perhaps she should have made him pay extra for it. As dearly as she made brunettes pay for their portraits, & other sitters with whom she felt little affinity of spirit.   —A certain lady on a high horse, who criticized the anatomy of her mount. Marie Laurencin threatened to repaint her on a camel.—

Perhaps Somerset Maugham joins the ranks of post-Apollinaire art critics, patrons & posthumous disparagers, who didn't think that a woman who "never was without a lover," & who liked to laugh, even in love, even at herself, could possibly have been a serious artist.

A PROPHET'S
(ONLY)
WIFE
EMMA
HALE
SMITH

July 10, 1804–   A young scryer named Joseph Smith
April 30, 1879   comes to Harmony, Pennsylvania, to
locate a lost silver mine for a farmer.
He boards with the family of another farmer, Isaac Hale, a fervent
Methodist. Whose initial hospitality gradually changes to contempt for the young scryer's professed powers when the lost silver
mine fails to surface.

    & to open dislike when the young scryer divines instead the
love reflected in the enormous hazel eyes of farmer Hale's daughter
Emma, the seventh & most regal of his 11 children.

    The faith receptacle created in Emma's mind & heart by her
fervent Methodist upbringing readily fills with belief in the eloquent young scryer. Who says that he is a prophet. & that he
talks with angels. She elopes with him, & marries him against her
father's wishes.

    Becoming a prophet's wife is to become his scribe.

    A scribe who is not allowed to share the visual manifestations
of the revelations her prophet-husband dictates to her. From
golden plates, whose hiding place   he tells her   was pointed

out to him by one of the angels who come to speak with him.

The prophet permits 11 of his disciples to weigh the plates in their hands. & he lets them glimpse the "reformed Egyptian characters" that cover them. Whereas his scribe-wife is only permitted to feel them through a cloth.

She protests. But how can she argue with a husband whose divine revelations turn into divine admonitions if she expresses a blasphemous opinion. A doubt. "Let thy soul delight in your husband," she is told, "Except thou do this, where I am you cannot come."

To be a prophet's wife is to bear small prophets. & to doubt her worthiness, & feel yet more sternly admonished, when her ·first 3 children die at birth. & to feel forgiven at last, when her fourth child   Joseph Smith III   survives his infancy.

To be a prophet's wife is to share her husband's poverty & persecutions. To nurse him, after he is beaten, tarred, & feathered in Kirtland, Ohio.

Which she flees, on foot across the iced-over Mississippi, with the manuscript of his *Holy Scriptures* sewn into her skirts.

But it is NOT to accept polygamy as a Law of God. Which is her husband's latest revelation.

Which he dictates to her.

Which she refuses to transcribe. & is instantly subjected to a divine admonition: "Receive all those that have been given unto my servant Joseph."

She refuses to receive them. & this time, for the first time, the prophet gives in. He burns his latest revelation   transcribed in his own hand, since she refused to write it down. It is a compromise between them, which allows her to ignore the new wives he continues to take.

Whose number reaches almost 50.

"He had no other wife but me," she proclaims, after the prophet is assassinated in Carthage, Illinois. For destroying the printing press of an anti-polygamist newspaper.

The rest of her   soon remarried   life is spent raising her years —14 of them quite alone, though famous— in her "fortress of meditation" in Southern France.

Where she relives her extraordinary journeys in the books she writes about them. Remembering them. Rehearsing her extraordinary findings: *The Secret Oral Teachings*. Translating old Tibetan manuscripts until her very end. —The head works well enough, only the legs refuse to go.— Until she dies at the age of 101, telling her housekeeper of a vision she's having of God the Father.

Who may have fused with her human father, in her mind's drift toward death.

She is 3 years old. & feels her father's arms hoisting her onto his shoulders, so she can get a better look at soldiers killing communards men, women, & children in the Paris of 1871.

He shoulder-rides her back to their house in the Paris suburb where she was born. Her mother is serving supper. Which she refuses to eat. Which looks like cooked pieces of people, in her plate. Her mother blames her father for taking a 3-year-old to see such things. Her father replies something about realities of life. Her mother says something else. & something else. & something else. Her father gets up from the table. He leaves the room. Perhaps he's leaving their house. She wants to run after him. She loves her father. Her mother stops her. She hates her mother. She wants to run away . . .

An impulse that runs like a thread through her next 50 years. Which she spends running perhaps from her restlessly searching self that always runs along.

4 5 8 times her parents catch her trying to sneak out. Where does she want to go? Where *can* she go? Unanimously for once her parents send her to school in London.

She still loves her father. A disillusioned pioneer of freedom, who has given up journalism by the time she comes back to Paris. She's in her early twenties. She picks up where he left off.

She still hates her mother. But it is her mother's condition the condition of wives & mothers she denounces in

4 prophet-sons in a fervently anti-polygamist version of the Mormon religion founded by her husband.

Eventually her group splits off, & becomes the Reorganized Church of Jesus Christ of Latter-day Saints, under the official leadership of her oldest son, Joseph Smith III.

Not unlike Martin Luther, or Henry VIII, Emma Hale Smith (Bidamon) became a religious reformer in protest against marriage regulations.

A CENTURY
OF ADVENTURE
ALEXANDRA
DAVID-NEEL

1868–1969   Adventurers   like the
                   are expected to die you
erably during an unfeasible feat, an impassable passage
swept mountains, that culminates in their spectacular

Survivors slink away into oblivion, hiding from the
of aging. Listening with age-muffled ears to the tales
about their spectacular youth. Their past.

Tales which often don't resemble what they rememl
often exaggerate   diminish   pervert what they
Questioning the authenticity of their quests, adulter
motivations.

Which sometimes upsets them. Sometimes to th
reappearing   a ghost-grey Casanova   to defend t
of their spectacular past. Which their unspectacular p
verts more than what the others tell about them. Old a
become adventure.

Yet, those who take great risks sometimes live on
Alexandra David-Neel. Who calls adventure her: onl
living. But outlives that reason, her last advent

passionate feminist articles. Until she, too, becomes disillusioned with so much bloodshed in the name of freedom.

Which obliges her to find a new, less conspicuous identity. Or rather: to change conspicuousnesses. She becomes an opera singer, hiding behind a stage name that makes her feel that: I is another. Even when Massenet compliments that other on the way she sings his *Manon*.

Which is not good enough to assure her a living in Paris at the turn of the century. The conspicuous ex-journalist turned less-conspicuous opera singer travels to Tunis, where she has been offered the position of "artistic director" in a casino.

—Which prejudiced ears may hear as meaning: the leading lady in a high-class Tunisian brothel. Where fiery women with British complexions & political Parisian pasts & Victorian manners notoriously attract the locally prominent.

Like the chief engineer of the Railroad.

Whose "taking advantage" of the by-now-32-year-old Alexandra David those same prejudiced ears may hear as meaning: the taking advantage of a chief engineer's   perhaps fleeting

desire by a currently destitute   perhaps desperate   adventuress. Currently in the skin trade, but whose true quest is truth.

Whose exquisite Victorian manners the chief engineer of the Railroad feels obliged   perhaps delighted   to marry.

Unaware that he is entering into a marriage of letters   — that lasts 40 years. Kneel, Philip Neel, to your itinerant wife.

Who promptly returns him to his bachelor life, as she returns first to Paris, & then to London. Where she toys with the occult, & seriously studies Sanskrit.

Preparing for adventures as yet unplanned.

Between 1904 & 1911 her letters to Philip mirror the as-yet-aimless quest of a mind rollercoasting on the brink of nervous breakdowns. Finally, in 1911, Philip offers to pay for a voyage to India. She is 43, & she promises to return within the year. When she will live with him.

For the next 15 years their marriage consists of letters from him, reminding her of her promise, alternating with threats to cut off her funds. & of her answers, which are new promises, passages of Eastern philosophy, & adventure tales. Which describe her continued journeys through:

India

Nepal

the Himalayas   —Where she meets   or traps   her restless self during one year of meditation in a hermit's cave, when she is 53. A year that passed much too quickly: she says of it later.

China

Japan

Korea

& finally Tibet, her most spectacular achievement. A journey so perilous & so unlikely   never before undertaken by a Western woman   that readers hesitate to believe what she writes about it in *My Journey to Lhasa,* after she finally returns to France in 1927. Famous suddenly, honored by the great minds of East & West who come to visit her in her "fortress of meditation" in Southern France.

Where Philip also comes to visit, often, reconciled with a wife whom courage & endurance have changed from a restless adventuress into a pioneer. A "lamina" who is perhaps a sage.

For 10 years she keeps still, writing books, translating ancient Tibetan texts with her adopted son, disciple, & travel companion Lama Yongden.

But in 1937 she's off again, with Lama Yongden. She is now 69, & this is her last adventure. This time to Peking, just in time for the Japanese invasion. They're cut off from Europe, like millions of other refugees, & spend the war years in a small town on the Sino-Tibetan border, writing, translating. Nearly starving, after Philip dies in 1941.

They're repatriated in 1944. They return to their "fortress of meditation." Where Yongden dies in 1955, while she lives on & on.

She refuses to pose for the medal the French government strikes in 1968, in honor of her 100th birthday.   —Old age does not become an adventuress.—   Obliging the engraver to rely on photographs of a younger   not so young: in her fifties   Alexandra in outlandish costumes & disguises. & of the gracious Victorian lady who always emerges after a mountain has been scaled, a border guard outwitted.

Who graciously takes tea with the princes, high lamas, gurus, & magicians she visits. & charms, convincing them of her knowledge & the sincerity of her quest. In their own languages, which she speaks.

She is the first Western woman to be received by the Dalai Lama.

She is also the first ever to enter Lhasa, the holy   forbidden   capital of Tibet. —Disguised as a beggar. Looking so authentic that she is beaten in the streets, like all common beggars in Lhasa.

These are the highpoints of her life. Her reason for living. The rest is anticlimax, if not meditation.

A DIFFERENT
ROSE
IN SPANISH
HARLEM
ALICE
NEEL

January 28, 1900–
October 14, 1984

In your vision of the world is the image of yourself.

Perhaps it was the year of her birth —the year 1900; in January— that programmed Alice Neel's commitment to the 20th century. *Her* century, whose age she shared year by year, until her death in October 1984.

Whose faces & bodies, conditions & institutions she painted, with a "professional single-mindedness that placed her in contradiction to a society which defined women by the male company they kept." Or, preferably: that was keeping them.

Alice Neel kept a great variety of male company. Her lovers came from all walks of life; yet another social defiance, but conformist-balanced by her strong sense of family. In her many portraits —of her mother her dead father her growing sons her daughters-in-law & of endless grandchildren— the single-minded artist merges with the daughter-mother-grandmother society expects a woman to be.

125

She married only once, a fellow art student from Cuba, Carlos Enriquez. With whom she went to live in Havana for a while

—Where she had her first exhibit. & her first child, a daughter, born after 8 hours of agony; who died a year later.—

with the feudal lords that were her husband's family. & later alone with him in various apartments. Dancing in the streets, & painting the "mulatto spirit" of Cuba. Which fascinated her.

It continued to fascinate her, & perhaps prompted her to move to Spanish Harlem, in 1938.

Long after the heartbreakup of her marriage. & the loss of her first daughter. & of a second daughter whom her husband took back with him to Cuba.

After a nervous breakdown, caused by the triple loss of her husband & the 2 daughters.

After several suicide attempts. & long desperate months of frozen volition in hospital wards.

—Which she painted, afterwards, when she was able to paint again, after she became "a highly trained neurotic," after her eventual recovery & release.

Of which she later said   —much later, speaking to art students a few years before her death—   that: "All experience is great, providing you live through it."—

After an involvement with a new lover, an ex-sailor who rekindled her energies. With whom she moved to Greenwich Village.

Who was an opium addict, & burned & cut up about 60 of her paintings, & some 200 drawings, in the winter of 1934.

When she seems to become more detached from her lovers, & more involved in politics. When she quotes Goya as her example that: An artist can be socially committed without lowering his level, as she sees herself more & more as a painter of "the human condition." Of what the world does to the men &   especially   the women who sit for her, often in the nude. Who are reactions to what the world has done to them.

She sees "sexuality as a social function," which she portrays in a male nude with tiers of penises reminiscent of a many-breasted Diana of Ephesus, or many-armed Indian goddesses. Or in a bloodless "Degenerate Madonna," or in endless pregnant nudes that bear witness to the "female situation."

Perhaps recognition requires detachment from the impression one makes on the world. & occurs   often posthumously when the artist's ambition is no longer focused on the effect a work might or should produce. When the work is free to speak for itself.

For Alice Neel, recognition came when she was in her late fifties. When she attracted notice & began to collect honors & praise. Perhaps it was then that the part of the canvas she always left unpainted, to allow the image "to breathe; to escape," escaped into fame while she was looking elsewhere.

Fame became her. The nude self-portrait she painted when she was 80, & photographs of her as a lovingly surrounded grandmother, show a woman not displeased with her "female situation." A woman whose life improved with practice, unlike the life of her contemporary 20th century.

DIVORCED
BY THE
DEVIL
MARY
MACLANE

May 2, 1881 –
August 8, or 7, 1929

What is it that isolates one daughter from the rest of her family. From her mother, her sister, 2 brothers, a step-father, who seem to be content, living in Butte, Montana.

Selfishness. She has cocooned herself in selfishness: chorus the mother/sister/brothers/stepfather. In the familiar unison that feels like an unscalable wall to the one   isolated   daughter.

Who protests: She's not selfish. She is not an egoist; she's an egotist . . .   & a genius.

It's my genius that sets me apart from the rest of you: she cries. Soundlessly, onto a page she heads: Today. Followed by 314 pages she heads: Tomorrow . . . Tomorrow . . .Tomorrow . . .

Which she covers with causes & descriptions of her bitter 19-year-long isolation among the seemingly contented. Of her exclusion from almost all of humanity. Except for Lord Byron. & Napoleon. & the Anemone Lady, the one teacher who was kind to her in school. The only person in Butte who seemed to un-derstand her, but then moved away.

129

I'm a philosopher! she cries onto hundreds of pages of tomorrows. I'm a writer, & a liar, contained in an admirable young woman's body!

Which I worship.

Which is adequately fed 3 times daily at the family table. & exercised   training the litheness of its admirable young woman's legs   during solitary walks through hours of Montana barrenness, & nothingness, & rock-strewn stretches of sand. Toward red-lined Montana sunsets.

& by doing housework. Training the elasticity of its admirable young woman's spine by scrubbing the familiar kitchen floor.

The bathroom, where the orderly row of familiar toothbrushes terrifies the genius/philosopher/writer/liar. Who is more truthful than the orderly contentment/the contented orderliness of the toothbrush owners. Who never seem to question the need for getting up   & eating 3 meals   & doing a little housework   & having a few conversations   & going to bed   & getting up . . .   Who are hypocrites, pretending to find contentment in the terrifying repetition of getting up & eating 3 meals & doing a little housework & having a few conversations & going to bed. Of being born   & growing up   & marrying   & bearing children   & dying   & being born   & growing up   & marrying . . .

Which she will not do. She will not marry! the genius/philosopher/writer/liar solemnly pledges to the bathroom mirror. Which reflects a solemn, plain-featured 19-year-old face. Redeemed by admirable hair, the color of glory.

Which the 19-year-old genius/philosopher/writer/liar craves more than anything in the world. Glory, the color of Montana sunsets, her very own red line of sky. Which would redeem her bitter isolation, her young woman's genius, misplaced in Butte, Montana. Where no one recognizes it; except the Devil. Who eventually comes to visit.

Bring it to me, Devil. Bring me my very own red line of sky.

For just one hour, and take all, ALL—everything I possess: she cries.

Prophetically; her glorious sky suddenly clouding with fear images of dying in a lonely hotel room.

On certain evenings the admirable young woman's body is alluringly clothed. With fresh stockings on its washed, walk-weary admirable young woman's feet. & the genius/philosopher/writer/liar goes to sit by the window of her room, to stare at the near perfection of ugliness all around her.

Perfecting her egotism until it becomes rare indeed.

Comparing the starvation of her young woman's soul to the seemingly satiated souls of the seemingly contented all around her. Who label her nameless wanting: greensickness.

Who are old, & raise age-thorned eyebrows   or young as she is, & stare at her with dead-fish eyes   when she tries to explain to them why her painful heart is made of wood.

Or when she says that she wears a necklace of turquoise & fire that has as many stones as her starved young woman's soul has had lives.

Or that, to her, sex is: a blest impediment   a celestial encumbrance   a radiant curse.

Or: that Christ has no humor.

Or: that her admirable young woman's brain is a workshop of the Devil.

In Whom she ardently believes.

Although she also believes that God is worth seeing. Although one can see Him only as one dies.

For over 300 pages of Tomorrows the genius/philosopher/writer/liar sits by her window, clothed in alluring anticipation of the Devil's coming.

He is a kind Devil, who understands her need for glory. & brings her her very own red line of sky, which lets her escape from the prison world of the seemingly contented toothbrush owners in Butte, Montana. & propels her to Chicago, & New York.

For one flaming-red year, that feels briefer than the one hour for which she pledged everything she ever possessed.

Which the kind Devil accepts in exchange. Leaving the dispossessed genius/philosopher/writer/liar to flail for a livelihood between bouts of drinking, & desperate gambling. Between Chicago & New York. Until one of the seemingly contented toothbrush owners travels east to find her, delirious with typhoid fever, & brings her back to Butte, Montana. To renewed isolation. & renewed anonymity. & renewed nightly writing   —after the fever leaves her body; less admirable, with no longer glorious   lackluster   hair.—   & renewed window-sitting, in anticipation of another visit from her kind Devil.

Who has, however, lost interest in the more & more rarefied egotism of the less-admirable-bodied, lackluster-haired, less & less young woman. Who has nothing more to give Him.

Whose nightly self-documentation takes on a whining tone.

Who finally flees Butte, Montana, for a second time. But this time isolation & anonymity travel with her. Back to Chicago. Where she had been famous   or notorious   for one red-lined year of glory.

Which fades further & further into the past, as the isolated anonymous woman becomes increasingly ill. & increasingly poor. Until it almost feels as though her one year of glory had never really happened. As though she had imagined it all.

Which she has NOT! She really was famous once. She really was a much written-about best-selling author, contained in an admirable, much photographed 21-year-old woman's body.

Whose glorious photographs & less glorious   disparaging   review clippings the 48-year-old woman arranges & rearranges in orderly rows on the dresser in the prophetic hotel room where she had feared dying.

Where she may or may not have seen the God she believed was worth seeing.

A POSTHUMOUS
INTERVIEW
ADÈLE
HUGO,
NÉE FOUCHER

1806–
August 27, 1868

Let me start out by clarifying that I was the first Adèle H. My youngest daughter was Adèle H. II. She attracted unfortunate notoriety when she fell in love with a married man who did not love her back. She followed him half around the world, until she went mad, & was brought back to France to live out her days in a mental institution.

I don't know how much of my daughter's tragic behavior should be ascribed to her growing up in the shadow of an overbearingly famous father. I can only state that madness ran in his family, not in mine.

& that living around him allowed for little personal space.

Victor Hugo was a part of my life for as long as I can remember. I can't think of myself without thinking of him. First. Not always lovingly, or even pleasantly, but always first.

We were playmates, he & his two brothers & I, since I was 9 years old. They'd blindfold me, & race me around their mother's garden in a wheelbarrow. Stop short & ask: Where was I? If I tried to peek they'd retie the kerchief so tight, I'd go home with bruises across my face.

They were still stupid then. 3 rowdy boys embarrassed to be playing with a girl. They'd try to scare me, & make me cry. Victor was the youngest, & the rowdiest. A real showoff. He'd set me on their swing & push me faster & higher, until I screamed to come down.

I think I liked Eugène better at first. I'm not sure. Maybe I felt sorry for him when he & Victor both fell in love with me at the same time, when we were all in our teens. When I realized that Eugène didn't have a chance.

Nobody ever had a chance against Victor. He always was The Victor, in school competitions, poetry contests, anything he set his mind on. He worked hard for it, of course, but it didn't seem to bother him if other people   —like Eugène, for instance— got hurt because of something he did. I don't think Victor ever said a word or made a gesture that didn't have a purpose.

& he really knew how to flatter.

I don't remember when I first noticed that he was obsessed with glory. It would help assure our happiness after we got married, he'd say to me.

He'd also say that he, too, wanted to be a virgin when we married.

Two unused bodies opening up to love & desire.

That was during the time of our courtship. I was living on a pedestal then, where his adoration placed me. I felt so high up & secure, I dared tell him what I thought & felt. That I didn't particularly care for poetry, for instance.

Although, being told/ in rhyme/ that I was noble & sublime/ that my eyes/ were stars in his sky/ my hair a cloud/ of thunder rolling loud/ within his breast; my lips/ a cherry, my lids/ pure gold . . . seduced me with the mirage of my own seductiveness.

We'd been seeing each other quite freely, at first. & we'd quarrel a lot. About little things, which he used to blow up into huge morality dramas.

I remember one rainy day, I was picking up my skirts not to get the hems all muddy, & he became indignant & lectured me about "showing too much leg."

Another time he kept harping on my friendship with the artist Julie Duvidal de Montferrier, with whom I liked to paint & to draw. "A fallen woman," he called her. He wanted me to stop seeing her.

Then he told his mother that he wanted to marry me, & she thought that her Victor could do better for himself than a petite Foucher. Despite her friendship with my parents, or perhaps because of it. She made sure we could no longer see each other, & he started courting me by correspondence. We were writing each other every day. He'd praise my fine style, & the original choice of my words. I, too, had the makings of a writer, he'd tell me. I'd believe him, & sit down to write him another letter.

Later, after we married & everything changed, he tried to seduce my friend Julie Duvidal. But her brother walked in on them, & stopped him in the act. Eventually Julie married Victor's oldest brother Abel, & we became sisters-in-law, & stopped being friends.

By then Victor had given up on his ideal of monogamy. At least for himself. & he was making up for lost time. Women seemed to flock to him wherever he went. To his name more than to his person, by then, I used to think. It didn't improve my respect for my sex. At least *I* had loved Victor before he became famous.

Although: Had I felt that he would become famous when I chose him over his brother Eugène?

Poor Eugène had been committed to a mental institution when he tried to kill himself, after I married Victor & not him.

& because of the success Victor was beginning to have with poems Eugène claimed to have written way back when both of them had still been in school.

Which may or may not have been true. Victor certainly never told me, & I certainly never asked. He suffered spectacularly on account of his poor institutionalized brother, but I couldn't tell if it was because he had stolen Eugène's poems & felt guilty, or if he felt embarrassed because of the stigma of madness suddenly attached to his name, or to his genes. Or if he grieved for the miserly sums of money he'd occasionally send for Eugène's up-keep. I used to think that he grieved mainly because of the money.

It was a hard fall from my pedestal into marriage. I'd realized during our early courtship quarrels that Victor had no sense of humor. But in those days I'd attributed it to his violent passion for me. Passion knows no humor. I started feeling differently about him altogether when I heard him boast that he had "possessed me nine times" on our wedding night.

I resented being "possessed."

& instantly getting pregnant. Again & again. I felt uncomfortable throughout, & my deliveries were horrendous. It spoiled my enjoyment of sex. The sensuality Victor later claimed I lacked.

Which he'd tell his various lady friends. Yet he'd have fits of indignation if I danced at a literary soirée. Unless I happened to be dancing with someone he thought might be useful to him in his career.

I had known from the start that Victor was devoured by ambition. But I hadn't realized how boring ambition would be to be married to. Stendhal & Mérimée found Victor boring also in his work. & Musset parodied his poems. But that was no consolation to me. I was carrying what was becoming a "resounding name," & I was too caught up in the sound effect to enjoy their making fun of it. They didn't live with him, or keep his house.   — For which I never had much taste or talent.—   They didn't have to sit with him every evening, while he checked what I had spent during the day. & why. Which he forced me to write down in a book, in meticulous detail. Calling me extravagant, because I'd bought a pound of early cherries to cheer little Adèle, who had been feeling poorly. He had no understanding for illness, or lack of energy. He could crack peach pits with his teeth. & of course he worked no matter what was going on around him. He was the measure of all things. A righteous judge who refused to tolerate my friendship with Sainte-Beuve.

In January 1831 he went so far as to offer to "trade me" to him. By the summer of that year I knew that I no longer loved Victor. I sadly agreed with what Balzac had written to his distant lifelong love Madame Hanska: That Victor & I were an example of what happened to lovers who got married.

Being a wife had so intimidated me that I felt stupid. Like a lining. I used to do pastels with Julie Duvidal during our adolescence. Portraits & flowers, but I gave that up when Victor started doing watercolors. & of course I'd given up writing completely during my first pregnancy, when I felt too uncomfortable to do anything.

If not, I might have been tempted to rewrite some of his seduction poems: His heart for me in longing ached/ he knelt before me & he sighed/ until he had me wed & naked/ to be assaulted day & night.

But that was no longer the case either. He rarely touched me anymore. Instead, a steady stream of ladies began climbing the secret staircase at the side of our house, to visit him allegedly unnoticed by the rest of the household.

Although he cared little about what we might or might not notice when his desires were at stake. He did not hesitate to take Léonie d'Aunet away from our son Charles. Who was 21, & devastated by the loss of his first love. I didn't know what to say to console him. I didn't feel that I could tell Charles that his father was a selfish tyrant   —Ego Hugo had become his "motto"— an abject flatterer & melodramatic miser, whose mistresses I pitied.

Especially one of them, a Madame Biard, who was caught "engaged in criminal conversation," i.e., having adulterous sex, with Victor one night in her apartment, & sent to jail. While he was allowed to go home, after claiming diplomatic immunity as a   very recent   Peer of France.

I went to visit the poor woman in her cell in Saint-Lazare,

where she was being held with prostitutes & thieves. & after her release I opened my house to her as to a friend. Which did not stop Victor from frowning on my friendship with Théophile Gautier.

Or from suggesting that I open my house also to another more or less established mistress of his, Juliette Drouet. I refused. Or rather: I delayed receiving Juliette Drouet until we were both close to 60. Not because I was jealous, but that woman seemed to have lost all self-respect in her hero-worship of Victor. She'd adoringly copy the manuscripts of her "great man," & correct his proofs, & be grovelingly grateful for the pittance he'd occasionally give her for it. & she wept with joy every time he took her along on one of his yearly trips down the Rhine, or to Spain. He hated to go anywhere alone.

It was during one of those trips with Juliette Drouet that he came across a local newspaper article describing the drowning of our oldest daughter. —In the arms of her young husband, who let himself sink with her when he couldn't save her.—

Victor rushed back at once, & grieved so spectacularly at the funeral that people started throwing strange looks at the rest of us, as though we'd had something to do with the young couple's tragic end during the weeping father's absence.

That he had to be the star even at our daughter's funeral drew me closer to the family of my dead son-in-law. Especially to Auguste Vacquerie, who remained a dear & thoughtful friend to me for the rest of my life. Which he made a great deal easier & more comfortable, renting a summer house for me at the seashore, or sending me fresh fruits & other foods, since Victor was still reluctant to keep me adequately provided for. Although he had become immensely wealthy by then, & I was getting quite old. I was suffering from dizzy spells & palpitations, & the vision in my right eye was dimming a little more each day.

Nevertheless I insisted on attending the opening night of Victor's play *Hernani* that was being revived for the Exposition Universelle in 1867. Victor was still living in political exile in

Guernsey　　—playing the destitute hero—　　& I wished for his name to be represented at the performance. Auguste Vacquerie accompanied me although he could barely walk. We were the blind leading the lame: he said . . .

Adèle Hugo died a year later. Her husband had her deathbed photograph enlarged & inscribed it: Dear Forgiven Departed.

The inscription on her tombstone reads:

ADÈLE

WIFE OF VICTOR HUGO

THE FABULOUS
REIGN OF
M A R I E
L A V E A U

V O O D O O
QUEEN OF
NEW ORLEANS

1783(?) to
June 16, 1881
to . . . 1918(?)

Papa Là-Bas is what Creoles call the devil. Affectionately: Daddy Down There. His emissary above ground is the holy serpent, bestower of "power" & "sight." The fatter the serpent, the greater the power.

Marie Laveau kept an enormous one in an ornate box under her bed. It fed on watermelons that grew on a vine in her garden, & she'd dance first on the box & eventually with the serpent writhing around her body, on St. John's Eve, when she led the yearly Voodoo dances.

She was a tall, stately quadroon   —a mixture of Negro, American Indian, & white. Her skin was dark with a reddish cast; banana-colored, according to others. Her black curly hair hung to her waist. It whipped around her shoulders as she danced, her gold jewelry jingling.

She was the first Voodoo queen to invite white thrill seekers, reporters, & the police   & to charge admission   when she assumed rulership in 1830.

& she was the only dancer to remain clothed. In a long ample skirt, the well-fed serpent coiling & uncoiling around a clinging bodice, her black eyes aflame under a *tignon*, a kerchief with 7 points sticking straight up, that sat on her head like a crown. It was obvious that she had the "power."

If you wanted to receive some of it, you needed to be "opened." You needed to strip off your clothes, drink *tafia*, a crude alcoholic beverage made from molasses, & perform certain rituals:

Rip a live rooster apart & drink its blood, letting it stream over your face & throat.

Skin a parboiled black cat with your teeth.

Slaughter a baby goat & eat its heart & liver.   —There was a rumor that Voodoos preferred a white child to a baby goat, if they could get one, & white parents used to scare unruly children, threatening to give them to Marie Laveau.

& then you had to dance. & dance. & dance until you dropped. Get up again & dance until you dropped. Get up again & dance. Until it was time to join in the sex orgy that lasted until dawn.

From 1830 on Marie Laveau had almost absolute power over the many-colored population of New Orleans. Negroes, mulattoes, & quadroons brought their problems to her all day long, believing that   like God, or Papa Là-Bas   she could give them love, wealth, & health, or make them suffer & die.

If you found a small doll stuck with pins on your doorstep, or a wax ball covered with feathers, you knew that an enemy had placed a curse on you.   —Voodoos always seem to have enemies.—   & you were doomed to waste away & die. Unless you could persuade Marie Laveau to lift the curse; usually by placing a counter-curse.

—There were many mysterious illnesses & deaths that baffled doctors & police inspectors. & it was rumored that Marie Laveau knew how to distill undetectable poisons from vegetables.

Her best-paying clients, however   —those who supported her alleged gambling habit, & made it possible for her to build her renowned *maison blanche*, the elegant white house on the edge of town, where white men met young "yellow" women, for a fee— came from prominent white families.

To whose secrets she had allegedly gained access while she'd gone to their houses working as a hairdresser, during her marriage to Jacques Paris, a free quadroon like herself.

He mysteriously disappeared after a year or two, & she began calling herself: the Widow Paris, as was the custom then.

Undoubtedly many of the white clients had told their hairdresser about many delicate situations in their lives, too delicate to tell their family & friends. Some of which she may have remembered. & undoubtedly much of magic relies on a good memory. But skeptics tend to exaggerate this discipline to supernatural proportions, while underrating the magician's other "disciplines."

Which the Widow Paris studied with the knowledgeable Voodoo master "Dr. John." —During the years she first lived with Louis Christophe Duminy de Glapion, another free quadroon. He moved in with her shortly after her husband's disappearance, & they stayed together until his death in 1835.

They had 15 children.

Who did not seem to have prevented the Widow Paris from surpassing her teacher. & becoming not only the great Voodoo queen Marie Laveau, but also the greatest mystic & healer of the Voodoo cult.

A matriarchal religion —despite an abundance of knowledgeable masters— which incorporates several Catholic saints in a power blend of so-called superstitions with accepted faith.

Marie Laveau prayed in the Cathedral for 3 hours, holding 3 peppers in her mouth, to assure a white politician's victory. For a very large sum. He won, & she was given protection from overcurious police officials for the rest of her life. People said that she had voodooed —or hoodooed— the whole police department.

As she grew older Marie Laveau began to visit prisoners on death row. Sometimes she obtained their pardon, hoodooing the judges. If not she'd take them a dish of homemade gumbo, & they'd die in their sleep, the night before their execution.

The greatest Voodoo queen of New Orleans is said to have ruled for almost 75 years, from 1830 to 1905. & here begins a conspiracy of documentation & counter-documentation that may be a deliberate attempt to create a legend of immortality.

If indeed, as records show, Marie Laveau was born in 1783 —there were a number of Marie Laveaus, born in New Orleans before & after 1783— she would have lived to be 122 years old. —135 years, according to people who claim to have seen her in 1918.—

She would have been 36 when she married Jacques Paris in 1819, close to 40 when she bore the first of her 15 children, & 47 when she ascended her throne.

Lafayette allegedly kissed her on the forehead. & Lafcadio Hearn allegedly was one of her lovers.

There is a rumor that Marie Laveau retired in 1869, but her queenship continued uninterrupted. A 42-year-old daughter, Marie Glapion, instantly took on her mother's name, deliberately trying to fuse —confuse— the famous mother with the aspiring daughter. A slightly lighter-skinned, rejuvenated Marie Laveau, with pupils shaped like half moons.

Which few people noticed, even when they came to her house. Noticing mainly that she was charging higher prices for her consultations, & that she preferred to hand out ready-made potions, instead of praying with them, & laying her hands on their pains.

Sometimes they'd notice an ancient woman sitting up on a bed in a far corner of the consultation room, with wild grey witch's hair hanging around a shriveled yellow neck. But they were too engrossed in their problems to pay her much attention.

Then there was a story that a Marie Laveau —the mother? the daughter?— had drowned during a storm after a Voodoo dance at her *maison blanche*. But 2 days or 2 weeks/2 months/ 2 years later she was found adrift on a log by a girl & future adept who took the near-lifeless woman home & watched in awe as she regained color & mobility.

& then, on June 16, 1881, a newspaper announced the death of "the Widow Paris," "a saintly woman who lived to be almost a century old."

Shortly thereafter, a Madame Legendre, another daughter of Marie Laveau —married to a white man, & almost white herself— allegedly drove the substitute Marie Laveau, & a Voodoo-master brother, John Laveau, from their mother's house.

Indignantly informing reporters & disappointed clients that no black religion, or magic, had ever been practiced in this house. That her mother had been a saint.

Which Marie Laveau may well have been. Forever repurified by the "Wash-Water" —Lave-eau— of her name. (In 1942 Father Divine allegedly offered $5,000 for Catlin's portrait of her, which he wanted to hang in his "Heaven.")

Just as the name Voodoo may —as some claim— be derived from Peter Waldo, the founder of the Waldenses — the French Vaudois— who were exterminated for preaching peace & helping the poor.

The spirit of Marie Laveau is still granting posthumous favors to those who believe in her: Knock 3 times on her burial slab state your wish out loud make a cross with a red brick, & you will be answered.

Attached is a list of her powders & potions available at the few reputable pharmacies which still remain:

Love Powder, white & pink	Moving Powder
Drawing Powder	Draw a Cross Powder
Cinnamon Powder	Flying Devil Powder
War Powder	Separation Powder
Anger Powder	Lucky Lucky Powder
Peace Powder	Good Luck Drops

Courting Powder
Delight Powder
Yellow Wash
Red Wash
Pink Wash
Black Wash
Lodestone
Steel Dust
Gamblers Luck
Van Van
Dice Special
Incense (Vantines)
War Water
Mad Water
Peace Water
Mexican Luck
Angel's Delight
Black Devil's Powder
Snake Root
High John Root
Good Luck Powder
Hell's Devil Oil

Mad Luck Drops
Extra Good Luck Drops
Fast Luck Drops
Love Drops
Drawing Drops
Luck Around Business
Robert Vinegar
French Love Powder
Get Away Powder
Easy Life Powder
Goddess of Love
Lucky Jazz
Come To Me Powder
Goddess of Evil
Love & Success Powder
As You Please Powder
XXX_3 Cross Powder
Lucky Floor Drops
Bend Over Oil
Goofer Dust
St. Joseph Powder
Controlling Powder

(VOID OF COURSE) THE CONTEST WINNER SNOW WHITE

1812 & Before— Fragments of a heartbreakingly beau-
Now & Forever After tiful girl-woman recur in many of the
folktales the Brothers Grimm spent
their lives assembling. Rearranging. Disentangling.

Isolating Snow White   —a desire fantasy of the perfect victim every man dreams of rescuing—   from Snowbella, Blanca
Rosa, Myrsina, Sleeping Beauty, etc. & especially from Cinder-
ella, whose excessive floor-scrubbing   —though excitingly de-
meaning—   disturbs the snowscape of pure helplessness with
thoughts of rough red hands & pails of dirty water.

Which belong to a different desire fantasy: Humiliation before
Redemption.

Snow White cannot be humiliated. She is an object   of desire   under glass. A sight, to pity & to covet. Almost without
a voice.

A motherless virgin
—Her real mother died giving birth to a wish dream that filled
her mind with a trinity of colors one winter night as she sat sewing.
—Whose fulfillment no real mother can survive.

147

Besides, alive she would deprive the story of its required villain.
A wicked real mother upsets the cultural image, whose projection
is the spontaneous source of most folktales.—

with skin as white as freshly fallen snow   —in which every
rescuer dreams of leaving the first & only imprint

a mouth as red as a fresh gash   —which every rescuer
dreams of inflicting; with a checkable trail on wedding night sheets

& hair as black as the Unknown   —in which every rescuer
fear-dreams of losing himself, while taking possession of the un-
knowable "Other."

Is it any wonder that the "wicked" stepmother wants to be rid
of this "spontaneous" fantasy of helpless purity/pure helplessness
that is obscuring the desirability of real women, like herself. It
has begun to eclipse her queenly reflection in the mirror eyes of
the men around her. Who are all dreaming Snow White. Her very
being feels threatened by this unfair competitor in the contest for
the fairest.

That has been going on ever since women lost their say, shortly
before the Trojan War. Which was caused by the first beauty
contest.

Since then, (sex) goddesses   Snow Whites   Cinderellas
      center-folded *Playboy* Bunnies   career-conscious Miss
Universes   have been competing for first place in the desire
dreams of men. Their judges.

But the ultimate judge is the mirror.

Which the threatened queen keeps consulting. Only to hear
the name of the contest winner repeated like a stuck record. The
heartbreakingly beautiful girl-woman seems to be indestructible,
despite the queen's elaborate attempts to do away with her.

Despite a total lack of self-defense on Snow White's part.

She meekly pleads for her life, but then risks it again & again
coveting trinkets: a poisoned comb   new corset laces   a red-
cheeked poisoned apple. Disobeying the wise advice of little
men.   —Collectively dwarfed by their desire dream. Whose

fulfillment turns the individual into a prince. Her rescuer.—
Otherwise she rarely speaks.

Her "wicked" stepmother, the queen, asks questions, & receives importune answers.

She protests, & schemes, & eventually she dies for it.

The dwarves sing, & sneeze, give wise advice, & go to work.

The princely rescuer whispers & coos.

Snow White just is. Objectified desire, comatose in a glass coffin. Unbeatably beautiful; & wronged.

But enduring. She will last to the end of men's imagination, or of literacy, whichever comes later.

The most assertive sound to come out of her is the choked gurgle as she upchucks the poisoned piece of apple.   —Whose red cheek is coated with her saliva, mirroring hundreds of tiny snow white lies.

Mirrors should reflect more deeply: demanded Apollinaire who always expected to see his poetry instead of his face.

OCT 16 '90 F

5/98" 11 5/98